Various Authors

Various Authors
The Fiction Desk Anthology Series
Volume One

Edited by Rob Redman

The Fiction Desk

First published in the UK in 2011 by The Fiction Desk Ltd

ISBN 978-0-9567843-0-8

The Fiction Desk Ltd
Registered office:
Office 404, Albany House
324 Regent Street
London
W1B 3HH

Please note that we do not accept postal submissions.
See our website for submissions information.

www.thefictiondesk.com

Printed and bound in the UK by CPI Mackays,
Chatham ME5 8TD

Contents

Contents

Introduction

Rob Redman

Back in the late nineties, just around the end of the big boom in alternative British music, I worked for a while as a DJ. I'd moved to a new city and hadn't found much going on there in terms of good music, so one evening I wandered into a club and somehow talked them into letting me run their Monday nights for them. For the next year or so, I played records from bands like St Etienne, My Bloody Valentine, and half the back catalogue of the 4AD label.

The club wasn't up to much: the beer was stale (but cheap), and they rarely replaced the bulbs in the lights, so there were times when the dance floor was lit for the entire evening by one meandering purple spotlight and an occasional burst of strobe. Both the turntables were broken and one of the CD decks skipped, so I'd put a long instrumental by Mogwai in the skipping one and use it to fill the silence while I quickly changed songs on the other deck. The crowd got used to hearing fifteen seconds of grinding guitars between each song, and occasionally losing half a Pixies chorus to a skipping disc. If there were complaints, a simple press of a button—under the decks, more or less where you'll find the panic button in a shop—would make the complainer, the dance floor, and most of the club disappear in a cloud of raspberry-scented smoke.

On some nights the club was packed, while on others it was so empty that I'd put on a compilation CD and sit down for a drink with the regulars. It lasted for around a year, before collapsing during a particularly quiet summer. It had never been a huge commercial success (one night we managed a door take of minus fifty pee), but it had a loyal following, got people listening to new music, and sold quite a few records. A few bands formed among the regulars, and some of those went on to record albums of their own.

Then, a couple of years ago, I started a book blog where I do my best to talk about new fiction. It's been a bit irregular, with some quiet months and some busy ones, but it's sold a few books, introduced a few readers to new authors, and given me the opportunity to meet some interesting people.

I like to think that the club night and the blogging both came from the same place: a desire to seek out new and interesting things, the worthwhile but perhaps overlooked, and to share them with as many people as possible.

One advantage that the music had over the blogging is that it was more direct: it was a case of 'listen to this' rather than 'let me tell you about this,' sharing experiences rather than simply reporting them. Much as I enjoyed rambling to people about why they should like The Magnetic Fields, I found that it was better just to put on the CD.

It's my preference for that directness that has led The Fiction Desk from blogging about fiction to publishing it: instead of boring you with why you should read Charles Lambert, or telling you to seek out Lynsey May's stories, or how funny the new one from Jon Wallace is, I'm just going to show them to you.

So go and grab yourself a bottle of out-of-date beer, find somewhere comfortable to sit (not too close to the toilets, if I were you), and get ready to hear some things worth hearing.

Oh, and please bear with any odd noises you might hear: it's not the music, just the CD player warming up.

Lynsey May's stories have appeared in The Stinging Fly, *as well as other print and online projects. She's also published a chapbook with Forest Publications, called* It Starts So Sweetly.

Two Buses Away

Lynsey May

It takes two buses to get to Ger's parents' house, and the second is always full of dickheads. His headphones are acting up too: there's a jittery buzz in the left ear that comes and goes at random and every time it flies in and over the music, his annoyance grinds a little deeper. It's his first day off in six days and he'd been planning to spend it in bed.

He's sitting with his knees shoved up against the seat in front, and has to twist and arch his back to get the MP3 player out of his pocket. Grunting, he flicks the switch off.

'You silly wee ho, you don't ken the first thing about me and Justine, you need to—'

He flicks it back on again. A spin of the wheel and he lands on some hardcore house. Ger looks blankly out the window for a beat or two before putting the player back in his pocket. The bass might complement the buzzing, even if it isn't likely to help his hangover.

The bus slowly suckers along the road, stopping, starting and lurching like a mechanised slug. He's got the seat to himself, but it's little comfort. He hates this fucking bus.

One of the girls from the gaggle on his left sprays a great swathe of cheap perfume. It's like the kind the girls in his high school used to wear, the kind that makes you think of sweeties and that's now making him think of Joanna Parker. He's not seen her around in years, but he'll not soon be forgetting the wee fleshy pyramids of her brand new tits.

She was the first girl in their year to grow any; for weeks the new tits had poked softly at the material of her school shirt and mesmerised all the boys. Everyone had been gutted the day she'd come in with a bra. Ger'd have liked the chance to see her in the buff some time, but by fifth year—when his face finally sorted itself out—she'd already been with two of his mates and was working on a third.

Ger picks at a stain he's just noticed on his knee. His best jeans and everything. Fucksake, that's a lecture just waiting to happen.

A proper old geezer is sitting a couple of seats ahead. Looking at the scrawny state of the bloke, Ger wonders what possessed him to haul his carcass up to the top deck. The top deck is for young folks: the youngest playing driver at the front; troublemakers strung across, and out, at the back; then there's the not-to-be-messed-with-but-decent-enough guys in the middle. The old guy is about a third of the way from the front. The collar of his jacket is so worn it looks wet in patches, and he stares out the window as though the view is worth looking at.

Ger thinks he can smell something bad wafting off him, a smell that piggybacks on the tantalizing spray of Joanna Parker and turns his stomach. He hopes he'll manage to eat whatever his mum has made for dinner. He hasn't had to leave the table to boak in a couple of years now, but the last time he did, he and his dad didn't talk for a good week or two.

Ger's been tensed for the first glimpse of the street for the last five minutes, but he doesn't move to slap the button until he's close to missing the stop. Before he stands, a bunch of wee radges from the back swarm past his seat, pinning him there and forcing him to wait. He ricochets down the stairs behind them. His steps and heart bounce to the beat in his buzzing ears and it feels good when his trainers hit the gravel and a light layer of drizzle coats his face.

One of the kids is shouting something, but Ger can't hear shit so he shucks his coat, sticks his hands in his pockets, and swerves around them. It's only when Ger's in the alley beside the park that his biceps unclench. Shithole, he mutters to himself. His folks are going to have to bite the bullet and sell up one of these days, before the house prices slide even lower.

There's no key in his pocket and the back door is locked. He yanks the earphones out and thumps on the patterned glass. The fresh silence makes his head vibrate. He waits for a handful of seconds, then steps round to look in the kitchen window with a phlegmy sigh, but the light's off. Back at the door, he leans one hand on the frame and makes a noise somewhere between a growl and a groan. The light comes on.

'Alright,' he says, straightening up at the minute. The old man opens the door and Ger looks down out of habit, expecting to see Suzie ready to wind in and tangle his step, but the cat is nowhere to be seen.

'Son.' Patrick shuffles back to let Ger in with the same nod that's welcomed him home since his first day at school. Ger slides by, holding his breath as though it'll also hold in the smoky smell he's realised isn't masked by the Febreze after all. His dad doesn't look at him, and Ger exhales triumphantly as he steps into the middle of the messy kitchen.

'Heya,' Ger says with a roll of his shoulders that slides his coat off. 'Where's mum?'

'Hang it up,' Patrick says as he closes and locks the door. His left hand worries the hair at the nape of his neck.

'She out?'

'Yes. Don't leave it there. Is it plastic or something? The radiator is likely to melt it. Hang it up.'

'Forget I was coming or something?' Ger says as he prises his feet out of his trainers. It was a short walk but the cuffs of his jeans are soaked and they flap coldly around his ankles. 'It was only the other day you called.'

'I ken,' Patrick says. 'Tea?'

'Aye.' Ger's voice trails behind him as he stops by the dining table to sling his coat over a chair. He can hear the whir of the kettle and sound of his dad chinking mugs as he shuffles through the stack of post on the mantelpiece. He leaves four bank statements and two credit card deals in the deck, but takes a plain white envelope to the sofa with him.

He's switched the TV on by the time Patrick appears with the teas.

'What's happened to the telly?'

'We got rid of the cable.' Patrick puts Ger's cup down on the wee table and then shifts it a little to rub in the circle of tea he's spilt. The sofa sinks beneath him when he sits: the springs are gone. The springs are better on the guest sofa, where Ger sprawls as he tears the letter open with half an eye still on the TV. Patrick picks up the cushion beside him then puts it down, picks it up again. He starts to roll his hand over its cover slowly; little tubes of cat hair appear at his fingertips.

'Fucksake, why do they keep sending me these?' Ger waves a student loan statement, a leftover from his first college attempt. 'Waste of time,' he says, folding it and jabbing it back at the envelope, then tossing it on the table. A corner lands in the spilt tea and starts to darken immediately; Ger can feel his dad looking, and also glances at the envelope, but neither of them reaches out to move it. Instead, Ger lifts the remote and aims.

'There's nothing on,' he complains as he clicks between the four channels, running through them one way and then the other.

'How've you been?' Patrick says with a chalky little cough.

'Fine yeah.'

'Busy?' he asks. Ger doesn't reply; he twists to look out the window instead, distracted by the fluting curses and brash laughs they can hear rollicking down the street.

'Little shits.' Ger says. 'Don't know how you put up with them.' He turns his head back towards the room. 'Not bad aye, got some extra shifts coming up.'

'Good, good, and that girl, Vanessa?'

'Ness. Aye, she's really good.' Ger says and he nods to himself as he picks up his cup and gulps the too-hot tea.

'So you're serious about her then? Ness, did you call her?'

'Serious, dad? Come on,' Ger says with a laugh in his voice but a kick of annoyance in his chest.

'Oh right, not like that then.' Patrick says, as he gently eases the knuckles of his left hand into a damp crack.

'Not like anything. She just...we're getting on just fine.'

'Good, that's good Gerry.' Patrick moves on to the right, massaging his knuckles in a motion smooth with practice. 'And you're doing okay at your work?'

'Aye, fine dad.' Ger says, his finger again racing the TV through its meagre channels. On the second lap, he pauses on a game of snooker. The two of them sit and watch quietly for a minute, lulled by the soft thunks of the balls and the chipmunk-chatter of the commentator. The relaxed atmosphere of hundreds of Sundays descends, filled with Patrick's clock mechanics and Ger's Warhammer models, framed by the hum of the telly. The memory is dispersed by a sharp yell from outside. Ger jumps and swivels on the sofa again, but there's no one close enough to see.

'Is it always like that?' he asks.

'Mostly.'

'It's a bit of a joke.'

Patrick makes a humming noise and Ger waits, but the inevitable speech about kids these days doesn't appear. Ger wonders if his dad is caught up in the snooker, but although the green surface and coloured balls are reflected in his eyes, Patrick's pupils aren't moving at all. Ger sighs a slightly rancid sigh and picks up the red top folded on the footstool. He skips past page three and scans the stories in the middle, holding the sheets up in front of him and snapping them straight again every time they start to wilt.

No mum, no dinner on the table, the house a tip—it's obvious they've forgotten. Waste of the bus fares, waste of his time, waste of a Sunday in bed. He squints at the news but hunger cramps quickly override his stubbornness.

'When's Mum back then?' he says from behind the paper. 'I'm starved.'

'Listen, Son.' Patrick's voice overlaps Ger's complaint. 'Your mum isn't on her way. You see, Gerry, I was wanting to talk to you. I've been meaning to talk to you for a bit. Thing is, there's this time in your life, this time when you've got to start admitting things to yourself.'

'What?' Ger says, a frown folding his brow.

'When you've got to look back on the choices you've made and take responsibility for them.' Patrick starts to nod, his hands planted on his kneecaps and eyes still trained on the TV.

'It's not always easy,' Patrick continues, and Ger shakes his head at the cheek of it—when he's been sorting the money out just like he said he would and everything. 'We all know it's not easy, no it's not easy at all, but that's no excuse now really, is it?'

'I can't believe you're going on it again, as though you've not listened to or believed a single thing I've told you.' Ger says. He realises his hands are shaking and quickly chucks the paper aside.

'What? What is it you're saying, Gerry?'

'I've learned my lesson alright? You don't have to keep bringing it up all the fucking time, I'm paying you back aren't I? Haven't I said thanks for it often enough?'

'It's not that, Gerry,' his dad sags further into the sunken sofa. 'It's me, it's your mum. I'm wanting to talk to you about what's going on with me and your mum.'

'What are you on about?'

'You see, your mum, she's saying...it's the drink.' The balls thud and spin on the TV and Ger's heartbeat makes him stay very still.

They sit facing each other on the same sofas they've always sat on. His dad is looking at him; it's all Ger can do to return his gaze. Finally, he blinks.

'I don't get it.'

'She's at her sister's.'

'So what? She's coming back though, right?'

'She's taken the cat.'

'And? What does that even mean?'

'I don't know, Gerry, I don't know.'

The buzzing in his left ear seems to have come back, but the headphones are folded in his pocket. Ger stands at the bus stop, dazed and shivering a little in his still-damp jeans.

He left his dad sitting in front of the TV, not watching a program about antiques.

'What are you looking at?' a squeaky voice says. Ger's stomach clenches. He focuses on the cap and marble-like eyes of the kid in front of him for a second, then looks away.

'You starting something?' the kid continues. Ger can't see his pals but he's sure they're there. They're exactly the kind of little pricks that make this place so fucking depressing, the kind who make your life a misery. Ger sets his teeth.

'All I'm doing is waiting for the bus,' he says.

'I'm no having people looking at me.'

'No one was looking at you.'

'Aye you were.'

'No one gives a fuck about you,' Ger mutters. The kid is scrawny but not wiry with it; Ger knows he could take him no bother.

'What're you saying?'

Ger squares up as he thinks about it. The kid's lip is curled and he is too young to hit really, despite his attitude. Ger swithers, but there's something about the boy's narrowed, amber-flecked eyes that makes him think of his dad.

'Nothing.'

You can learn a lot from fiction. For example, this debut story from Londoner Harvey Marcus is a handy cut-out-and-keep guide to...well, to falling in love with an air hostess.

How to Fall in Love with an Air Hostess

Harvey Marcus

Begin by getting on the fifth carriage from the front of the 10:36 from London Paddington to Cardiff Central on the 10th October, 2008. Bundle your coat onto the overhead shelf, and take your seat. Listen to music, waiting twenty minutes for the train to pull out. Gaze absently at the empty platform for some time before you notice the pretty girl in an air hostess uniform sitting diagonally across from you. Sit up straight, and try not to stare. Think of something to say.

In the event that you cannot think of the perfect thing to say to a beautiful stranger on a train, try to visualise some common ground between you. Put yourself in her size six black pumps with silver buckles. Get under her slightly too-small blouse and skirt with thigh bulge. Walk the cabin. Close overhead compartments. Glance at seatbelts. Tear open steaming packets of food. Ensure your seat backs and tray tables are in an upright and locked position.

Do not smell the food. You can't be hungry yet, or can you? What time is it meant to be? From where we were, or where we're going to?

That's your first question: 'What time zone are you in now?' Not a bad opening gambit, and much better than the 'Where've you just flown in to?' that the ticket inspector has just tried. He gets a polite, non-committal response: he's quite fat and old.

Don't ask yet, though. An opening gambit does not a conversation make. Squeeze back under the orange blush skin, wriggle the ends of your fingers till your nails slip under her perfectly manicured half-moon cuticles. She flew in to Gatwick, she says to the ticket inspector. And now she's going to Cardiff. 'Quite a commute,' you might say, 'do you enjoy travelling generally, or just on planes?'

No no no, that's shit, what are you talking about? Planes or trains, it's all the same basic aisles, same seats filled with bored passengers, Styrofoam food and untouchable scenery. She doesn't care about that, she's had a long flight, all she wants to do is get home. She definitely does not want to talk about travel, literal or philosophical. There has to be something of interest to her you can talk about, but you only have the vaguest outline of what an air hostess actually does. They unpack the food, then...

Before you even have time to pull the Hammer for Use in Event of Emergency and hurl it at his pudgy grey head, this ticket inspector has stolen your line. 'Quite a commute,' he says, even in the tone you would have used – a little ironic, a little teasing, getting in on the joke. 'Like travelling, don't you love?' Love! Has he no shame, you think, doesn't he know how ridiculous he looks, a man of his years chatting up a girl like this, with you sitting here, young and available. Fat old bastard, leave some for the rest of us!

Clearly this won't be as easy as you first thought. Persevere though, really get into the role of air hostess. Empathise in a major way.

What first interested you in the role of air hostess? Well, I have an extensive background in the service industry, I was just born to make people happy. Yes, I enjoy all kinds of work, I love meeting new people. It's kind of glamorous, isn't it? Years ago, my mother sent my sister and me a postcard from one of her long trips away. We got many of these and most were nothing special, but this one had a beaming air hostess in front of a plane. It was sleek against a perfect blue sky, like a polished silver bullet. I thought she was the most glamorous woman I'd ever seen, and somehow I got the idea that my mother was an air hostess, and that this was her giving us a little slice of her life. The woman in the picture had a navy blue blazer with gold buttons and a navy blue pillbox hat. I hid the postcard in a shoebox under my bed, and when my sister asked where it was, I told her I'd lost it. At night I would get it out and stare at her perfect features: her perfect strawberry red lips and perfect white teeth, eyes like blue drops, blonde curls in an exact style. The perfect woman.

Yes, I used to serve food in my part-time job at uni. Media Studies, that's right. A third.

Now that you think about it, do you need to go to university to be an air hostess? No, she would have been one of the go-getters who dropped off the education-into-spiralling-debt radar and was already earning unbelievable amounts of money (to you at least) by the age of nineteen. Stuff your gap years, she's off to Milan! New York! Sydney! Bucharest! snatching all the highlights within a bus ride of her Holiday Inn before it's off to the next place, all on the company payroll. Yes, she was clinking drinks with a braying Home Counties co-pilot in Athens International while you were back here, scribbling 'Man vs Nature', 'Juxtaposition' and 'Irony' in the margins of the Penguin Classics edition of... whatever. She's a high flier, she's cruising at a different altitude, inhabits a different plane—

n.b. avoid all plane jokes. At first sign of such a joke, bail out immediately.

Regain focus. Find some common ground.

You must be able to find some common ground. She's pretty and you're...well.

Go back in time two hours and shave. Clip nails. Shower. Moisturise, deodorise, sanitise. Leave house. Get on train. Completely by accident, sit across from air hostess. Think of something to say. Say it. Say something to her. Whenever you're ready.

Go back ten years. Walk slowly out of the cinema with Lizzie Spooner, letting your friends go ahead. Kiss her when the coast is clear. Go out with her for a personally significant but not life altering period of time. Break up, or get broken up with. Feel traumatised. Grow.

Repeat with the others you missed. Grow more. Live a regret-free life. Act quickly, think decisively, and vice versa.

Shit, shower, shave. Moisturise, deodorise, sanitise. Leave house, sit across from the pretty air hostess on train, don't notice her for a half an hour. Then notice her. Then say something. Anything.

You might like to know at this point that you are now approximately halfway through *How to Fall in Love with an Air Hostess*. Consider how you are doing so far. You might wonder whether the window of opportunity (to put it coldly, for a 'romantic encounter') is now shrinking perceptibly. You count forward how many pages you have left: you are in fact a little over halfway now. Console yourself that if the window of opportunity is shrinking, at least it is not any further away. You avoid wondering if there is any difference by continuing to think of something to say.

You do have plenty to say, if you could only get rid of this bloody ticket inspector. Listen to him talking about his daughter, who flew with Virgin Atlantic for a while but now has her own café. Well la-di-fucking-da. You envision some Greasy Spoon in Hackney, serving glistening heart attacks to vulnerable builders with above normal blood pressure. Extra hash brown with that, mate? Refill your hot brown water, lovey?

Do not show signs of reaction when you realise you know the place. An independent coffee house near where you live, with floor-to-ceiling bookshelves and baristas who serve good hot espressos that aren't absurdly expensive. The counter is loaded with homemade cakes; you have to have the carrot, it's too good. The woman behind the counter says it like she's just eaten some herself, not as if she's selling you anything, and you get some. She's got brown hair, coffee brown in fact, tied back with a pencil stuck through the bun. She turns her hips and torso in a way you like under her white shirt, and she has a broad, generous smile. You trust a smile like that.

When she brings over the espresso you exchange a few words about the book you are suffering. She likes it and you tell her you don't, even though it's the truth. Then you're stuck on the one page for ten minutes, running through *How to Fall in Love with a Café Manager*. Then you close the book, get ready to go, walk to the till and pay for the drink, pay her even though there are other staff there and it could have been any one of them, and she's giving you your change and looking pretty great. You say thank you, and she says something back, 'You're welcome,' maybe, but you have your music on so you don't know. Then you leave.

The ticket inspector has stopped talking at last, comes up to you and punches your ticket. When you take it back from him, he's looking at you and winks. Is he saying 'Your turn'? Or perhaps, 'You see that? Never too old.' How repulsive, you think. How unflattering to all concerned.

Clearly, this isn't going to work. You're just not The Type. If the world was sorted into your type and The Type, there would be a high, padded wall between you. All those brash, confident, unfeasibly beautiful people and ticket inspectors mixing together and having the best parties and the loudest conversations, and your type on the other side, putting up with the rhythmic thudding and the sound of cheering every time someone dropped a glass. They're madder than March hares over there, you whisper to the person meditating next to you, and they all fuck like rabbits.

There she is, alone now, reading a text while running a hand through her too-good-to-be-real hair. Is life, when you think about it, too short? That's what they say at least. One thousand months long, if you're lucky. The thought used to sober you, but how many of those have you passed happily enough? Neither wasted, nor crushing every opportunity out of them until your arms shook, just lived.

Final destination call, five minutes, and you have almost finished *How to Fall in Love with an Air Hostess*. Please ensure that you have all of your personal belongings with you on leaving the train. On behalf of Harvey Marcus, we would like to wish you a safe and pleasant onward journey. While it is not recommended at this point to try a last-ditch effort to catch her attention, you may go for it anyway. A moment of eye contact perhaps, or a murmur of "Excuse me," as you reach for your bag overhead. If she looks at you, ensure that you smile winningly. You are now on the very knife-edge of possibility with this woman, and the tiniest wobble will undo you. If by some cosmic confluence of miracles she smiles back, or engages with you in any way, forget everything you've just read here. You don't need that kind of excess baggage, you'll be lucky to get in even one question as it is. So make it a good one. Something simple and engaging. Something quirky but not weird and off-putting. Something that doesn't sound like you've been preparing it for an hour, that doesn't sound like you at all. Something like...

'Where have you just flown in to?'

Ben Lyle is a graduate of the creative writing MA at the University of East Anglia, but is also one of our contributors with a background in film: he's worked with the UK Film Council and Working Title, and is now co-head of development at Gorgeous Films.

Crannock House

Ben Lyle

Which of these definitions is correct?
Beriberi:

a)   A Mexican sauce
b)   An ailment of the nervous system, caused by
         malnutrition
c)   A Sri Lankan siren
d)   A Malay word for 'friends'

I can't look at those word games in the newspaper without thinking about Mervyn. If you guess right, you can pretend you knew the answer all along. They have them in all the papers now, but back in the mid-eighties only *The Times* had it, on the back page next to the crossword.

On the first day of term one year, I was sitting alone in the school dining room and reacquainting myself with colourless porridge and kid-cut toast, spread thinly with St Ivel Gold and thick honey. Short and fat-faced, I must have been thirteen but I was already an old hand at the school, one of about fifty boarders. A large steel teapot stood on the table, looking like the head of the Tin Man. Pouring a cup, I turned to the window and gazed out over the gravel, past the sloping football pitch towards the meadow. Grey, green, greener and then again grey: the low dark grey of the troubled Scottish sky.

A strange man marched across the gravel in front of the window, his face determined and serious. His hair was spread out across his shoulders and down his back. His beard reached from his nose to the top of his chest and stretched from ear to ear unchecked. Amid the inky bushes of his face lay two ale-dark eyes and a swollen red nose. He looked like an escapee from *The Muppets*.

'It's the yeti!' shrieked Jenny, a mole-speckled girl my age.

'Hey! Don't be rude.' Fran, the history teacher and part-time cook, sat down. 'That's Mervyn, the new maths teacher,' she said in her Canadian accent, sounding American but not.

'He's dressed like a teacher,' I said. 'I hope it means he can count.' He wore proper trousers and a Marks and Spencer-style jumper over a shirt and tie, barely visible through the thatch. This was not typical wear for the staff at my school. That morning Fran, for example, wore clogs, flared orange trousers and a fringed poncho.

In the educational world, Crannock House School was known as 'progressive'. There were no compulsory lessons: learning was considered a contract between teachers and pupils. The idea was that children knew what was best for them. My parents thought I'd do well in an environment of joy and discovery, rather than set texts, exams and school uniforms. That's what my dad wrote in his articles for *The Guardian* anyway.

It wasn't a rich school. Most of the kids got benefit help and many had been chucked out of other schools. Crannock

House became the last resort. Located on a small estate in the Scottish countryside, the school worked at utopia with a bunch of misfits. I was the exception: my parents had the money to send me elsewhere but they were ideologically committed. I imagined them boasting at dinner parties about their only child's idyllic schooling, whilst I was four hundred miles away from London, saving them money on babysitters and learning nothing.

The whole school would meet once a week, ostensibly to run the place. One of the older kids chaired the meeting. Even the ageing headmaster, his sporran resting in the lap of his kilt as he leant forward with hand raised, had to wait his turn to speak. My dad described it as a revolutionary way to engage children, but in reality the meeting dealt with tedious admin: who left the cowshed door open, can people remember to put their dishes away after tea, will Billy undertake to stop calling Ka a chipmunk?

On the first day of term the meeting was always a short one. It was only September but someone had wheeled out the Calor gas heater. Its warmth disappeared into the rafters of the purpose-built octagonal hut while the smell hung about our heads. At the end the headmaster introduced Mervyn and said how lucky we were to have a Cambridge man. Mervyn gave a quick nod and saluted with his biro. It was only when we filed out that I realised he'd been doing the *Times* crossword all along.

'Can you teach me how to do those,' I said, pointing at the paper as we walked away from the Octagon.

'I'm here to teach you maths,' he replied without breaking stride. He stretched out the vowels when he spoke, like my cousins from Bristol, that I hardly ever saw.

'Go on, give us one clue at least.' I followed his nervy movements. He looked down without stopping.

'I don't encourage fraternization,' he said.

'Is that the clue?' I hurried to keep up with him. 'It sounds like gobbledegook.'

'It is not gobbledegook.' He laughed and looked directly at me for the first time. 'Nor is it a clue.' His face sharpened for an instant, like a stoat or a weasel in *The Wind in the Willows*. 'Good word though,' he continued. His eyes blinked as if helping him clear his head. 'Now leave me alone.'

The first lesson we had with him was a shock. He expected us to be quiet, for one thing. Before then, every class had been a free-for-all, a debate about what might or might not be worth learning about any particular subject. In Mervyn's class we sat quietly whilst he explained Pythagoras' theorem.

'You already know what the length is,' Billy said. He pointed at the blackboard 'It says it's Z. Look.'

'Z's an unknown.' Mervyn scratched at the board. ' X, Y and Z—they're all unknowns.'

'But if they're all unknown, how do you find them out?' Billy persisted. He was thirteen too but we didn't speak much. He wiped his snub nose, adding to the silver spindles on his sweat-shirted forearm.

'It's not real,' I said. 'It's a theorem. The measurements don't matter.' I glanced up at Mervyn.

'That's right,' he said, stepping nimbly to the side. 'Here are the set questions for next week.' He gestured with a chalk-scarred hand.

'You mean we have to answer all those?' I asked as I folded away my exercise book. I was quite pleased: I'd learnt more in one lesson than in the previous two years at the school.

'Brilliant.' He smiled. 'You're obviously the brains of the class.'

'I have to work in my own time?' I said.

'That's why it's called homework,' he replied, and ushered us to the door.

'But it's a boarding school. I won't be going home for weeks.'

'Don't be smart.'

'If I'm not to be smart, how do you expect me to do the sums?'

'They are not *sums*,' he said, faking anger. 'They are equations.' He pursed his lips for a moment, then shut the door.

I used to catch sight of Mervyn striding about the grounds or starting off to the pub three miles away. He walked with quick, jerky movements that sliced through the air, always alone.

'What college did you go to?' I asked him one day at lunch.

'*Which* college,' he said, pumping salt into his bowl. 'Maudlin. Spelt M-a-g-d-a-l-e-n-e. Oxford has a college with the same name but without the final E. After Mary Magdelene.'

'Who's she?'

He spluttered. 'She's in the Bible!' He looked at me for a moment then slurped up the spilt soup from his beard. 'Haven't they taught you anything here?'

'This school's not religious,' I said. 'Unless you count blind faith.' I gestured at the kids around us.

'Blind faith indeed.' He smiled. 'Is there any other kind?'

'Will you show me how to do the crossword?'

'No,' he said, getting up to leave.

'Please?'

'It's not a good idea, it really isn't.'

The rest of the school bored me senseless. None of the teachers knew much and the others were just kids. I didn't really have any friends. In the end, I ignored what Mervyn had said, and went to see him anyway. His cabin was made out of chipboard and perched on a breezeblock base at the end of a row of converted brick farm buildings, like the last outpost of a hilltop station. Beyond it lay the school's small farm, with its three horses, two cows and a fat sow that squealed once a year when it littered. Chickens pecked at my feet as I banged on the door.

'What do you want?' he said, standing in the doorway.

I held up my exercise book. 'I've got a couple of questions about the homework.'

'Can't it wait until class? You really shouldn't be here.'

'It'll only take five minutes,' I pleaded.

'Very well.'

The cabin was even more basic than my dorm. The low-slung bed was a tangle of grey and brown, like a pile of winter coats. An armchair, a stool and a wooden box doubling as a table completed the furniture. A notebook lay open on the box. As the last of the October sun mottled one wall, Mervyn drew a ragged curtain. He rested on the edge of the stool and pointed me to the armchair.

I picked up a completed crossword from the chair and sat. 'Why is this "mood"?' I read out one of the answers.

He poked fiercely at the smouldering fire, trying to cajole the damp logs into life. 'What's the clue?' he said.

'Condemnation about atmosphere.' Smoke drifted as much into the room as up the chimney, making the place feel strangely windy rather than cosy.

'Easy,' he said. He poured a glass of Gaymers Original Cider from a green plastic bottle as he explained the solution. 'But what about the homework?' He triple blinked.

'What are you doing here?' I asked. The smell of cider mingled with the choking smoke. His hand gripping the poker reminded me of an over-cooked chicken wing, all bone and stretched papery skin.

'Trying to get the bloody fire started, what does it look like?' Resin bubbled and water hissed out of the wood as the fire grew hotter.

'I mean here, at this kind of school.'

'That's a big question,' he said. He ran his fingers through his beard but didn't answer. A tangle of horsehair came away in my hand and I realised I was tugging at the arm of the chair.

'What's this?' I picked up the notebook from the table. It showed a list of names down one side, with numerous dots against each name and a corresponding number on the other side of the page.

'It's a cricket game I invented,' he answered. 'It's played with dice.'

'Have you been playing against yourself?' I asked.

He nodded as he finished his drink, *ahh*ing in satisfaction.

'Will you teach me?' He looked doubtful so I grinned at him. 'I'm here now.'

Much of the rest of that winter I spent round Mervyn's. There was nothing to do in the evenings and it was always dark. The school was miles from anywhere and didn't even have a television. I always went alone. We used to look at the word game in the paper, go through the crossword and play dice cricket.

'I had beriberi once,' Mervyn commented on the word game one day.

'You were starving?' I asked, confused.

'No.' He stood up and went to the shelf over his bed and scrabbled around for something. I realised I'd never seen him in a change of clothes.

'You can also get it from excessive alcohol consumption. I collapsed in Montrose high street,' he continued with a crooked smile. 'At eleven in the morning. My mates in the pub opposite thought I was pissed.'

He sat down and drank from his glass. 'I spent six weeks in intensive care,' he said and laughed, as if remembering an exciting scrape from his childhood: caught scrumping apples.

'Is that why you left your last school?' I asked, prying apart another piece of kindling with a billhook.

'No.' He looked at me in an odd way, then picked up a length of rubber tubing and started fiddling behind him. His hands shook.

There were a series of tubes and plastic bottles all leading to a large, dirty barrel on the floor. 'What's that?' I said.

'Homebrew kit. It'll have to do until pay day.' He put his lips to the tube and sucked, spluttered then plunged it into one of the barrels.

> *Which of these definitions is correct?*
> *Jazzer:*
> *a)*   *A slang term for an upper-class cricketer*
> *b)*   *A 1920s groupie*
> *c)*   *An irresistible temptation*
> *d)*   *A malicious spirit*

When you saw him from afar, Mervyn seemed quite big and imposing. His huge head of hair made him look like a dirty lion. But his body was actually very slight. He barged into me one day when we were scuttling into the Main House to get out of the rain. I couldn't believe how frail and bony he was.

'Move it,' he said as he squeezed through the door. 'I'm getting soaked.' His midriff brushed against my back. He stared out across the gravel.

'Why don't you buy a coat?' I said.

'On my wages?'

Sometimes when he was off at the pub I would sit in the kitchen of the heavy grey stone Main House, leaning against the massive Aga, sniffing the lentil soup and warming myself while Fran cooked dinner.

'So tell me about Mervyn's cabin?' she said as she sliced potatoes. 'Is everything okay?'

'What do you mean? He's a friend.'

'But what do you *do*?' She put down the knife and looked at me hard, her head to one side. The kitchen lights flashed off her thick glasses.

'We play games and talk,' I said. 'He knows stuff.'

'I know stuff too,' she laughed.

I stirred the soup with a steel ladle. 'Why do you work here?'

'Oh God, I don't know.' She moved the chopping board aside. 'I like kids, I guess. It's rewarding, watching them learn, seeing them work things out for themselves.'

'Mervyn's like that too.'

'Oh, he's fine,' she said. 'Just as long as you're okay?' She pushed away from the table and turned to the walk-in larder, like a boat putting out to sea.

At the end of that first term, Mervyn posted the maths test scores on the school notice board. There was uproar. A couple of the kids were in tears. Fran comforted Billy because he'd scored badly. Jenny didn't care at all, she said, about 'stupid maths.'

'That's because you can't do it,' I replied.

'Shut you face, James. We all know you're his pet.' She flounced off.

It didn't bother me. I was top of the class anyway. The staff hated the idea that the kids might be competitive. I overheard one of them muttering to Fran that the headmaster took a dim view. The tests didn't stop, though. 'Competition makes everyone better,' was all Mervyn said on the subject.

He even sent school reports to our parents, with the test scores on them and marks for effort. It was the first report anyone had ever written about me. It said:

The presentation of James's work has improved
vastly. The manner in which he mishandles a pencil,
however, still leads me to conjecture that he has
ambitions in the field of applied archaeology.

That summer we built a cricket net on what was called the grass
tennis court–though I doubt anyone had played tennis there for
at least a hundred years. In the first weeks of term, it was still
overgrown and permanently damp. We found an ancient roller
discarded and rusting beneath a tangled briar and set about
preparing a practice wicket. It was hard work but I didn't mind.

Mervyn told stories about Gloucestershire County Cricket
Club and how he'd followed them as a boy. He wore his beard in
tribute to WG Grace, he said. I became so used to these stories
that when we finally got to play I couldn't believe what a poor
player he was. A wiry medium pacer, he could never put any real
zip on the ball. His technique with the bat was okay but his eye
terrible. He would play a classical straight drive, but somehow see
his middle stump uprooted all the same.

I was a much better player. As a bowler, I had real pace. Once I
hit Mervyn above the hip with the ball. He pulled up his jumper. A
blue-green mark appeared on his side, a round bruise the exact size
of the cricket ball. It was a shock to see the sallow, strangely creamy
skin of Mervyn's stomach. I felt queasy as he hopped around.

'Bastard,' he said. 'Good delivery.' He was pleased I gave
everything. I could tell by the way he picked up the bat again, and
said, 'Bowl.'

The school was too small for its own team so we got involved
with the local club. I was good enough to play with adults. My
mum sent up some new whites in the post. Mervyn would turn up
in his black trousers, with a white shirt so dirty it was impossible
to believe it had ever been washed. It had large seventies style

lapels and frills down the front. I changed in the small pitch-side hut that doubled as a pavilion. He always used to get in the way, his arms, legs, and hair everywhere.

'Give us a bit of room will you?' I said as I pulled my flannels on, my back bumping against him.

'Sorry.' He stepped away.

'Careful,' I said. 'Who're we playing this week?'

I let him chunter on eagerly as I finished getting dressed. He didn't have anyone else to talk to, so sometimes his words spilled out.

Mostly we were in the same team but occasionally we played against each other. Mervyn kept wicket and sledged all his opponents, chatting to the incoming batsman in order to put him off. I couldn't believe it when he did it to me the first time I came out to bat.

'Ere comes the pretty posh boy,' he shouted to his fielders in an exaggerated West-Country accent. 'E don't like it up him.'

I took guard and settled in to face my first ball when I heard him whisper. 'Go on ya jazzer, smack it through the offside, this bloke can't bowl.'

'What's a jazzer?' I thought, just as the ball came down. In confusion I slashed at it and missed by a mile. Behind the stumps, Mervyn leapt up in ecstasy.

'Howzzzat?' he screamed, claiming the catch.

'I never touched it!' I stared back at him in disbelief, only to see a weasel grin cracking through his beard. The umpire had given me out.

'You cheating bastard,' I said as I trudged off. 'You know I didn't hit it.'

'That's cricket,' he replied. He never looked happier, sweat-damp hair stuck to his forehead, large lapels flapping, one catch to the good.

On the hot journey home, fumes leaked into the minibus and I sat behind Mervyn the whole way, inhaling the petrol mixed with his stale cider and exercise odour. I knew he wasn't going to wash, either: his cabin had a darkly stained hole of a toilet and a cold tap.

'Do you fancy coming round after dinner?' Mervyn asked as we arrived back at school. 'Finish the England-West Indies game.'

I looked away, back towards the soft squares of light burning out of the Main House. He twitched a glance down the farm track, his unlit cabin just a dark shape in the distance. 'You can have the armchair,' he offered. 'I'll stay on the stool.'

'No,' I said finally. 'I've got stuff on.'

> *Which of these definitions is correct?*
> *Nutant:*
>
> *a)   Pliable*
> *b)   Easily fooled*
> *c)   Lonely*
> *d)   Drooping*

It was a long summer holiday. I grew four inches waiting around. I spent most of the time watching test cricket on TV, except for when my parents took me to Greece. Mervyn had taught me some ancient Greek, but it was useless in Skiathos.

As soon as I got back, I headed round to his cabin. Everything felt smaller. Mervyn seemed like that, too: I looked down on him slightly, could see how flat the top of his head was, how thin his arms looked. The cabin felt claustrophobic as we chatted about the cricket season. The rank, rotten smell was even worse and I coughed a couple of times, my legs too long for the cramped room. More plastic barrels had appeared in the corner, the homebrew kit growing at Mervyn's expense.

I wasn't the only one that had grown. Some of the girls dressed differently and were beginning to change shape. Jenny's face had lost its roundness but her body had compensated. Her dark, half-Spanish eyes obsessed me. I soon found a chance to sit down next to her in the art room.

'Wow, that looks great,' I said, as I leant over her shoulder and tried to see beyond the dark mole on her breast. 'Who taught you how to do that?'

'Oh, I tried some stuff out for myself,' she said, pleased that I seemed to like her experimental block printing. 'You don't always have to be told how to do things, you know.' She smelled like fresh fruit and vanilla.

'It's dewberry,' she added offering her wrist.

I thought her so sophisticated. Only later, shopping with my mum back home, did I realise that half the fourteen-year-olds in the country wore dewberry. That was the problem with the school. You didn't know anything about the real world until you went home.

Hanging out with Jenny was fun all the same, and we began doing stuff together after school hours. I lost interest in Mervyn's games. It wasn't that Jenny did anything special; things were just different. I don't know why, but not much else seemed to matter except her.

One day in maths she drew a bear on her exercise book, with a big M on its stomach. I laughed.

'Be quiet!' Mervyn rasped.

'Sorry,' I said rolling my eyes at Jenny as he turned his back.

'Now, James, what's the quotient of this matrix?' He asked.

'Pi,' I replied. My eyes slid back towards Jenny. 'A nice juicy steak and kidney pie.' She giggled along with everyone else. Mervyn looked at me with disdain but said nothing.

'James, wait a moment will you?' he said as we filtered out. 'We're still friends, I hope?'

'What do you mean?'

'You can't behave like this in class,' he went on. 'It's disrespectful.'

'I was just having a laugh,' I said. 'That's all.'

'Will I see you at the cabin?' He shuffled papers in front of him and avoided my eye. 'It's been a while.' He waited.

'I don't know, maybe,' I said. We both looked at his hands as he held the limp paper before him. I noticed purplish dirt under his nails. 'We'll see,' I whispered as I closed the door, unsure what else to say.

I didn't go round there that night, but I saw the next morning he seemed to be a bit wobbly. His dark eyes were bloodshot like something out of a comic and his hair totally awry. I called out to him as he walked across the courtyard but he didn't hear me. For some reason, I was glad.

A few weeks later—I still hadn't been round to the cabin—he tried to hand my exercise book back but he couldn't grip properly and it flopped on the desk in front of me.

'Absolute rubbish,' he said. I looked at the mark.

'Fifty-five percent? That's not bad.'

'You should be doing much better.' He wiped the board clean. 'You've found more interesting things to do, I expect.'

'No. No, I, er.' I didn't know what to say. 'Maybe we can go through it tonight?'

'It's your marks I worry about,' he said, ignoring my comment as he turned. He stood close to me and I smelled the alcoholic vapour that hung between us.

'Have you had a drink?' I laughed. 'It's not even lunch time.'

'How dare you say that,' he growled, and then, 'I thought you were my friend.' He fell silent as if ashamed.

No one had ever called me their friend before, not as if they really meant it anyway. I looked away, embarrassed, as he slumped onto one of the classroom chairs. I thought about thanking him, but that didn't seem right. In the end, I left without saying anything.

The other kids liked Mervyn as a teacher but out of school hours, they kept clear. Whether it was the smell or the hair, I don't know. After the summer, a fresh crop of young kids had arrived, and they found Mervyn approachable. They started going round there once I'd stopped. They'd seen me visit him a few times at the beginning of term, I guess, so it must have seemed normal. I couldn't understand what he saw in them.

Near the end of term I overheard some of them talking about how crazy Mervyn was, and what a laugh they had at his cabin. The next night I went round after tea. I was curious to see what all the fuss was about.

The cabin was packed with eleven-year-olds. Frantic stringed folk music strained out of the tape recorder and the room was hot with smoke and cider. Mervyn barely acknowledged me. He was too busy beating his feet to the music. His eyes flickered wildly and I could see he was already well into a second bottle of the Gaymers. A couple of the new girls tickled each other on the bed, screeching. A small boy sneaked a sip from Mervyn's glass but he snatched it back.

'Oi! That's mine you cheeky bugger.' They both laughed. Mervyn took another gulp. 'Get your own.'

A new, even faster song came on. Sissy, a dark-haired girl who had a habit of turning her chin into her right shoulder when she talked, stepped over to the machine and turned up the volume. Mervyn followed her with his eyes. 'What's Lothario doing here?' he asked. She looked up at me for a moment.

Mervyn leapt to his feet. 'Let's dance,' he shouted, grabbing her hand.

The two of them whirled around in a ragged circle while the rest of the kids screamed in delight. Mervyn grinned, his eyes askew as Sissy squealed in excitement, 'Too fast, too fast.' As the song reached its conclusion, the two of them stumbled and fell onto the bed, scattering the girls. The children's laughter filled the silence at the end of the song. Mervyn gurned at me. I got up to leave.

'Too much, is it?' he snapped, gesturing for one of the kids to pass him his glass. 'Not enough girls to go round?' His voice raised, he went on. 'Round girls. Go girls, girls go round, girls, round girls,' he shouted over the hysterical cries of the children.

'It's not—' I began.

'Who let you in anyway?' he rasped. 'I never asked you to come round. I never asked.'

'Watch this,' the small boy yelled as he tossed a plastic bottle into the fire. It flamed up, all blue, white and green together. I left them staring at it, the smell of burnt plastic caught in my nose.

A couple of weeks later I came down the stairs to the kitchen and caught sight of Sissy in the staff room just as the door swung to. Her head was bowed low, a band of white scalp running lengthways down her crooked parting, pale and obvious against her lank black hair. It wasn't long after that Fran came looking for me. She never normally came up to the middle landing, but on the last Monday of term she knocked on my door.

'What's going on there, James?' She didn't even say hello.

'Going on where?'

'Not now, James.' She sat on the bed and began again more softly. 'At Mervyn's place?'

'I haven't been round there for ages,' I said. 'I don't know what you're talking about.'

'If you're keeping anything from me—'

'I'm not, honest,' I pleaded. She got up but turned back at the door. I wanted to say something else.

'Don't worry about me,' I offered, finally. 'I can look after myself.'

'It's not always about you, James,' she said sadly, and left.

The following term, Mervyn was gone. He had been given the sack. The kids called a special meeting to force his reinstatement. He was still popular as a teacher. A couple of the oldest kids spoke up for him, saying it was unfair to fire him without consultation. The headmaster remained unmoved. He said only that it was impossible for Mervyn to stay on.

'Are you going to say anything?' Billy looked across the Octagon and I realised the whole meeting had turned to me. 'He's your friend,' he continued, exasperated. I thought of crossword clues. I thought of Mervyn slumped on the classroom chair, saying 'my friend'. I thought of his slender hands and a cramped cricket changing-room. I looked at Sissy's nutant head and all I could think of then was: too fast, too fast.

Rumours went round about why he'd been sacked but I kept quiet. I didn't say much all term. I didn't want anyone blaming me for anything. Fran evaded my eye whenever I entered the kitchen. Jenny tried to bring me out but I'd somehow had enough of her. All she wanted to do was talk. For some reason, I couldn't stop thinking about Sissy. I'd catch sight of her around school but I could never look at her for long. Her greasy hair repulsed me and the sight of her sloped shoulders heading into the dining-room made me sick.

A year or so later, I was on the Glengowan bus back to school when Mervyn boarded. He looked possessed, eyes cavorting as he swung down the aisle. He was rancid drunk. I knew the signs by this time, had even been pissed myself. Sunlight levered through the windows as the coach pulled away.

He sat down a few rows in front of me, but his smell soon crept along the bus. It took me straight back to his cabin, the reek of unwashed armpits and stale cider, of unbrushed teeth, rotting one by one. It was so familiar and so disgusting at the same time that I couldn't believe I used to stand it.

'Christ man, that's reekin',' someone muttered. I glanced back at two shaven headed boys in tracksuits. One of them sharpened his face at me for a moment, then nudged his mate.

'It's giro day, so it is.' The friend laughed.

'It's no right,' a woman called out to the driver. 'He shouldna be allowed on. I cannae breathe.'

Mervyn mumbled and created shapes in the air with his hands. His clothes looked dirtier than ever and his hair was uncombed. He had once taken pride in brushing it with a fork but he had given up even that. I knew he lived in a caravan about two miles further on. He'd been living there on the dole since he'd left the school but I never visited him.

A couple of others spoke to the driver but no one spoke to Mervyn. An exclusion zone now marked out his space in the bus. My thighs squeaked against the plastic seat.

'He's paid his fare,' the driver said from the corner of his mouth. 'Jesus.'

The bus made it to the next stop at the Bridge of Dee and a couple of the younger lads shouted again at Mervyn. Get off, ya dirty bastard you. Away to yer bath. Some women added to the protests until the driver turned in his seat, looked at Mervyn then stared at the open doors and waited.

It was only one more stop. I was big enough by this stage to say something. I could have sat down next to him and got him home.

Been his friend. No one would have argued. It was because he was on his own.

When they send you off to school, your parents tell you that you'll make friends as if that's a good thing. They don't tell you the flip side. I sat still and waited like everybody else.

Mervyn finally got the message and stood up. He mouthed unintelligible words to the passengers, then his eyes caught mine. For a second I thought I saw a flicker of recognition, a moment of stillness. Then he mooed, like a Tex Avery cartoon character, before stumbling to the door. As we drove off I scrambled to get another look at him.

He was muttering to himself but as I looked back at his bedraggled figure disappearing in the bus's rear window, he shouted quite clearly, 'I never asked you to be my friend. I never asked.'

Stories often seem to arrive at our office in thematic batches. One day will bring lots of difficult divorce stories, another will involve a series of alien invasions. On the day I read 'Rex', I'd already seen three or four stories about man's best friend. This one stood out, though I can't think why...

Rex

Jon Wallace

Rex opened the front door, carefully poking his head into the house. When he was certain it was clear he crept inside, tip-toeing his way to the kitchen, being sure not to wake Sylvia. She slept all the time now, which was fine by him. Her waking hours were not a good time to be around. She was still depressed about Ernie.

A month ago Ernie had been hit by a car out on the street and killed. Sylvia mourned that dog as if it were a relative, which Rex understood. But the other night she'd implied Rex had been complicit in the mutt's death. This struck a nerve in Rex, and there had been an argument. Hadn't he been the one to find the dog? Hadn't he been the one who brought the stinking carcass back into the house, cradling him in his arms as if the wretched pup were some fallen general? Didn't he get any credit for that at all?

Of course, he knew where she was coming from. He had never liked the dog, and it had never liked him. He had resented paying more for the Sir Lunchalot gourmet dog food than his own dinners. He had resented the dog's attitude: Ernie only ever regarded him as a rival, certainly never as a master. Finally, he had resented the hound's persistent invasions of the bedroom, where it had always done its very best to prevent cordial marital relations.

He was stood in the kitchen, thinking over these things, when he heard something odd. It was the sound of Sylvia coming in through the front door.

What is she doing up? he asked himself. She had passed the last three weeks without leaving the bed, let alone the house.

He went over to the kitchen door and listened. There was something strange going on: Sylvia was talking to someone. There was something in her speech that wasn't right. There was too much joy in it. He thought the voice a little unhinged.

Oh God, he thought. Is she talking to herself now?

There was a scratching noise, as if Sylvia was slipping about on spiked trainers, and she was laughing—*laughing*—at something. Crossing himself, he made up his mind to go into the hallway and greet her.

He tossed open the door with a flourish, raising a smile he in no way felt, and took in the sight now greeting him.

Sylvia stood looking at him with wild, wet, and joyful eyes. She was, in spite of being drenched, considerably more attractive than she had been for the last month or so.

But she was not alone.

Snuffling around her feet on all fours, panting and emitting small growling noises, was a man in a dog costume.

There was a silence as Rex examined this man.

He was wearing some kind of home-made fancy dress costume. His face was fully exposed, apart from a rubber snout on a string that he wore over his nose. On his head he had a novelty headband, sprouting black felt ears. On his torso he sported a loosely fitting body suit, torn in several places and flecked with Dalmatian spots. On his hands and feet were the remains of black socks. Finally, sticking obscenely out above his rump, was a black wire tail. The only vaguely authentic thing about him was his brand-new, black, metal-studded collar. Sylvia was clutching the leash tight in her fist.

The dog-man had been scampering about until Rex entered, but now noticed Rex. His eyes widened and he became very still, apparently unsure of himself.

Rex said nothing. The dog-man didn't say anything either, but his expression suggested he hadn't foreseen Rex's presence.

'Well,' said Sylvia finally, 'What do you think?'

Rex remained mute. He couldn't stop staring at the man in the costume.

'Rex?' said Sylvia. 'Don't you like him?'

Words still eluded Rex, but he didn't want to create a situation. He had to say something.

'Who's this?' he said, a slight crack in his voice.

'It's our new dog. He's called William,' said Sylvia. 'Isn't he beautiful? He's a Dalmatian.'

'Really, a Dalmatian, eh? Well, I never,' said Rex.

He edged over to the coat stand and wrapped his fingers around the handle of an umbrella, drawing it out slowly, clutching it like a broadsword ready for action. William regarded every movement anxiously.

'Where did you get him?' asked Rex. It was a good question, but he hadn't meant to ask it. The most important issue at hand was that Sylvia appeared to believe the man in the costume to actually be a dog. This, coupled with the fact she had been leading a man on a leash around the neighbourhood, caused Rex some thought. It didn't seem to concern Sylvia.

'I placed an advert in the local paper asking for puppies,' she said, 'and this little lad turned up at our door this morning. I think his horrible owner must have abandoned him. Well, he's no puppy, but I think he's perfect. We'll take care of each other, won't we?' she said to William, and crouched down to embrace him against her bosom.

Seeing this affection, Rex released his grip on the umbrella and considered.

While Sylvia's behaviour was doubtless irrational, she was at least smiling. He had not seen her do that in close to a month. True, there was something in her smile that suggested not all was well within, but what were his options? It might be dangerous to reveal William's humanity to Sylvia. He didn't know what she would do if he brought her crashing down to Earth like that. She might well wear the same smile while she beat him and William to death with a table lamp.

Better, Rex thought, to let her down gently. Play along for now and give himself time. He would drop some hints, make a few suggestive comments. She would get the picture when she was ready. Perhaps this would help her through the trauma of losing Ernie. God knows, something had to.

Then, of course, there was the small matter of the dog-man's motives. What was in this for him? Perhaps he could be dealt with. Rex resolved to find out.

'Well, an orphan, eh?' he said. 'I suppose we can make room for a little while.'

Sylvia seemed happy with that. At least, she was still smiling.

'Come and pat him then,' she said, beckoning Rex over. 'Say hello to William.'

Gritting his teeth, Rex approached the man-dog, reaching out his hand as if performing some cruel initiation ceremony. William looked Rex right in the eyes, equally concerned by this development. Rex patted him on the head a couple of times. The suit had the texture of Velcro, or cheap floor covering.

'There,' said Rex, shivering in horror, 'consider him patted.'

'Oh,' said Sylvia, shaking a reproachful finger, 'I don't think that was a proper pat. I think Daddy is a bit scared of William.'

'Oh, God,' said Rex.

'Do you think he's scared of you, William?' said Sylvia in a baby voice, 'Do you think Daddy's frightened of you because you're such a big boy?'

At first the man-dog seemed delighted with the compliment, and smiled a little as Sylvia nuzzled him and pressed his face to her breast.

Then, suddenly, she leapt to her feet in jubilation, yelling:

'Come on, William, let's go for a run!'

She bounded towards the living room, tugging on the leash, causing it to tighten instantly around William's neck. It garrotted him violently, and he was pulled onto his back, tugging at the leash for air. It took Sylvia a moment to realise what had happened.

'Ooh, dear,' she said. 'William?'

She released her iron grip on the leash, allowing the man-dog a little oxygen. William gasped, wide eyed, but quickly recovered himself. He transformed his tongue from a pained appendage that had almost been dislodged, to the cheerful, lolling pant of man's faithful servant.

Nevertheless, Rex thought he should step in.

'Look, Sylvia, why don't we let him run about a little, eh? Let him find his way around the house.'

As soon as he said it, Rex realised that the man-dog's entire act could in fact be a scheme to burgle the house. Bizarre and elaborate, yes, but he could not dismiss the thought entirely. He decided to send the dog into the kitchen, where there was nothing of value.

'Go on, William,' said Rex in as friendly tones as he could muster. 'Go have a poke around the kitchen.'

William appeared to register something in Rex's eyes. Panting excitedly, he obligingly bounded into the kitchen, giving a little woof as he went for good measure.

'Look at that, he understands you!' said Sylvia.

'So he does,' said Rex. Quickly he closed the door, locked it, and pocketed the key. 'Now why don't we get you upstairs into a hot bath before bed?'

'Ooooh, but I want to get to know William!' she said.

Rex grabbed her by the shoulders, and stared deeply into her eyes. 'I want to get to know him too,' he said. 'But we've got all the time in the world, baby.'

'Oh, Rex,' she said, resting her head on his shoulder. 'You really like him?'

'I really like him,' said Rex, kissing her on the forehead. He stroked her hair for a while, holding her face into his chest, and silently mouthed some words that were best not heard.

When he was certain that Sylvia was sleeping, Rex pulled the covers off his pyjamered body and fed his feet into his slippers. The green digits on the alarm clock read twelve twenty-two. He sat for a moment to listen, but heard nothing. The house was quiet. After a minute he went out into the hall, closing the bedroom door behind him, and made his way downstairs. The kitchen light was on. He could hear the kitchen TV and could smell cigarettes.

He took a deep breath, turned the key in the door, and walked in.

William was seated in one of the red plastic chairs, watching the football highlights. He was still wearing the dog costume. On the table next to him was a glass of beer and a mug, which he was using as an ashtray. He glanced up at Rex and raised his palm lazily.

'Evening,' he said.

Rex strolled into the room as casually as he could, switched on the kettle and leaned on the counter.

'So...' he said.

William did not reply. He appeared slightly irritated by Rex's presence. Then something happened in the football and he leapt a small way out of his chair, before sighing and reclining back into his seat.

'Nearly,' he said to the TV.

'So,' said Rex again. 'Who are you?'

The man-dog put out the cigarette he was smoking, but immediately sought out his pouch of tobacco and began rolling another.

'I'm your dog,' said William.

Rex shook his head.

'No, you're not my dog. You're really not a dog at all, are you?'

'Yes,' said William.

'No, be honest now,' said Rex.

William put the tobacco pouch aside and rested his chin in his hand. He looked at Rex, considering something.

'I am your dog when I'm in character.'

'In character? What does that mean?'

'It means I'm an actor,' replied William.

'An actor?'

'Yes. I'm a damn good one too.'

The man seemed perfectly serious.

'But this isn't a theatre,' said Rex. 'This is my kitchen.'

'Hey,' said the man in the dog costume, suddenly affronted. 'I don't need a theatre. I don't need a director and a producer and a script, yeah? When I play a part I live it. I am it. I don't need a seated audience to understand a part and commit to it.'

Rex didn't feel that the man-dog had a right to be upset by the question. He was, after all, drinking his beer and watching his television.

Rex poured some hot water into a cup, added a teabag, and scooped in one sugar.

'I don't mean to cast aspersions on your talent,' he said, 'but can't you get a better part than this?'

The dog-man lit his cigarette.

'I know actors who would kill for this role,' he said. 'People have threatened me for it. They've said: 'I'll kill you if you don't give me that role."

'Things are that bad in your profession?'

'Things are tough,' replied the dog, nodding gravely. 'But that doesn't mean this isn't a challenging part. Any thespian worth his salt learns something from every dramatic role.'

Rex was a little frustrated by the conversation. He felt the need to establish his authority.

'Well, be that as it may, it seems to me that I have a stake in this production of yours, providing, as I am, the venue? So I think you and I had better have a little chat.'

'Sure,' said William. 'Whatever.'

Rex settled himself in one of the chairs opposite William and stirred his tea with a spoon, looking at the cigarette burning in the man-dog's paw. Small chunks of ash lay on the tablecloth. William had flicked the cigarette only in the general direction of the coffee cup.

Rex pressed his thumb and forefinger to his nose and sighed, gathering his thoughts.

'The situation is that my wife has been very depressed,' he said.

'Yeah,' said William absently.

'Yeah? What do you know about it?'

'She told me,' replied William.

'She's been talking to you? She thinks you're a dog, doesn't she?'

'People talk to their pets, believe me,' said William.

Rex was confused.

'You've done this before?'

'Oh, yeah,' said William. 'This is my third dog gig now.'

Rex found that his train of thought had escaped him. He decided to start again.

'So anyway, as I say...Sylvia has been very depressed, and I think that your presence, whatever your motives, may be beneficial to her recovery. You see, we had this dog before—a real dog—and it was hit by a car in the road, and it has affected her badly. I think having a kind of placebo dog could work very well. Perhaps we can agree to continue this...arrangement until my wife is back to her old self. Then, I'm afraid, the curtain must come down on your performance.'

William narrowed his eyes at Rex and rolled his cigarette between his fingers, considering the proposition.

'So...you're on side?' he asked.

'Yes. Well—I'm not paying you or anything. You can eat out of the fridge, I suppose...'

'Oh, no, dog food will be fine,' said William.

'You'll actually eat the dog food?' said Rex.

'Oh yes. I'm in character for twenty-three hours a day. You've caught me during my break, you see. All the rest of the time, I am one hundred percent dog.'

'Fine, whatever you like, but you will speak to me if the situation allows, do you understand? I'm not going to ask you questions and be barked at, get it? There'll be no Lassie act.'

'You're asking me to break character,' said William.

'Only if it is absolutely essential that we communicate. Think of it as asking for a prompt, or an intermission. Whatever. But if you want me to play along, you will have to consent to my terms.'

William rolled his tongue around the inside of his mouth, considering.

'Agreed,' he said finally.

Rex offered his hand to shake on the deal.

William looked at the outstretched palm for a moment, then grasped it in his paw and shook vigorously.

'Deal,' he said.

'And for God's sake repair that costume,' said Rex. 'I can see your pants through that thing.'

At first, it was a gratifying arrangement for all concerned.

Sylvia returned to her old self. She was out and about during the day and considerably more amorous during the night. It was particularly pleasing to Rex that, unlike Ernie, William left them well alone in the bedroom, using the time as the ideal moment for his hour-long TV and cigarette break.

Rex found William particularly useful in providing a window into the workings of his wife's mind. Aspects of her thought processes that had previously been hidden were now revealed. When she returned from a walk with William, the man-dog could provide useful intelligence into Sylvia's thinking and Rex could react appropriately.

When Sylvia told William that Rex had not taken her out to dinner in a while, Rex could respond that very night with an evening of gourmet delights, fine wine, and dancing. When Sylvia recounted a particularly bad day at work to William, Rex could light scented candles, play whale music and treat his wife to a massage. Best of all, when she wished to be left alone, Rex actually knew about it and could take advantage. He visited the cinema alone, or went to the pub with the lads, or walked in the park, safe in the knowledge that it would earn him no reproach.

The longer it went on, the more Rex felt himself to be the luckiest husband on the planet. No other spouse enjoyed such access to his other half's mind.

Of course, there was the odd awkward moment. For one thing, Sylvia was not always in the mood to take the dog for a walk, and insisted that Rex do his fair share in the parental responsibilities.

'Take William to the pub with you,' said Sylvia one afternoon. 'I'm sure they'd all love to meet him—he's such a handsome boy.'

Rex was nervous at the suggestion, but William gave a few reassuring woofs, and off they trotted. Rex tried to creep into the pub and conceal the dog in a shady corner, but found to his amazement that the punters all wanted to come over and say hello to the hound. They patted and stroked William, and said approving things about his teeth and coat, and asked about possible Crufts categories, and remarked on how friendly he was to strangers.

'I must admit, you're very good,' said Rex as they strolled back that first night.

'The trick is thinking like a dog,' said William. 'If you think like a dog, people see a dog.'

There were only a few elements of the subterfuge that Rex found testing. William would regularly lick his intimate parts on the carpet, in plain view. He would pick fights with other dogs. He would run off into the distance when let off the leash. He would howl to be let outside, and then immediately howl to be let back in again. He would bark at his own reflection in the window.

Yet these were small things, and were, as William regularly explained, all in keeping with his character.

When the big problem finally did come, Rex cursed himself for not anticipating it.

He was reading by the fire one evening, William curled up at his feet, when Sylvia returned home from work in a state of considerable excitement. She sat down in the armchair opposite Rex, clapped her hands together and grinned the too-wide grin.

'I've had an idea about William,' she said.

'Yes?' replied Rex.

'I think we should breed,' she said.

William opened his eyes a little but, pro that he was, gave no other sign of alarm. Rex was not nearly so composed.

'Breed? What do you mean, breed?'

'Well, I've been thinking that William is such a handsome, fine specimen—everybody says so, don't they? So I thought we could get a bitch for William and make some puppies. Everybody's doing it! You can make lots of money. And we'd have lots of little ones running about the place. William would have his own little family!'

Rex looked at William, and William looked at Rex, and employing the telepathy they had developed over the past months, they agreed on a position without saying a word.

'I'm not sure. It sounds like it could cost an awful lot in Sir Lunchalot, wouldn't you say?'

'Oh, bother that—we'd make it all back selling off the puppies!'

'But...but what if he's not in the mood? After all,' he said, seizing on an idea, 'it's winter. He won't get frisky until spring, will he?'

Sylvia stood up and raised her hands for quiet.

'Rex, I won't hear another thing about it. I've been thinking about it and we have to do it. We simply have to.'

She ran over to him, and kissed him on the forehead. Then she leant down to William, and pulling his face to her bosom, exclaimed:

'Oh, William, isn't it wonderful? You're going to be a daddy!'

Unsurprisingly, Rex called an emergency conference that night, held in the kitchen as always. He crept down the stairs at three, leaving Sylvia with dreams of puppies in wicker baskets.

'Look,' said William, 'This is trouble. She's going to find out.'

'You're right,' said Rex. 'This is bad.'

'I mean, she willingly suspends her disbelief all right, but for how long? Bringing in another dog could really damage the credibility of my performance.'

They sat quietly in thought for a few minutes, until a thought came to Rex.

'I don't suppose...I mean, if you really are a method actor...are you saying you wouldn't even consider sniffing its behind a bit... making out you're not interested? I mean dogs don't necessarily go for whatever is presented to them, do they?'

William exhaled ruefully.

'I'm afraid so. Dogs don't turn down sex. Besides, I know your wife. She won't stop trying, even if it means her sitting there and watching me mount the other dog.'

'And you wouldn't do that...?'

'No,' replied William.

'I thought you said you had to "think like a dog"?'

'Look, I'm an actor, not a German porn star. Besides, it might bite me or something. Think of something else.'

There was more anxious debate, and for a while it looked as if there was no solution. Then, finally, as the sun rose gracefully over the early morning traffic, a plan was hatched.

It went thus:

Rex would tell Sylvia that he agreed to use William to breed, but only on the condition that the project would be his to carry out, and his alone.

Rex would then purchase a female dog, pretending that this bitch was on loan from some reputable breeder. The bitch would be brought home and left alone in the kitchen with William, and the pretence of a coupling would take place. Rex would explain to Sylvia that, having read up on canine courtship rituals, he knew it to be essential that the dogs were left alone together for a successful courtship to take place.

Then, at a later date, when Sylvia was out of the house, Rex would simply fake the birth of puppies by purchasing a batch from the same place he'd bought the bitch.

After that, it would simply be a matter of taking the bitch to the nearest pound, and selling off the puppies as quickly as possible. It might mean taking a loss, and it might mean the house being full of real, irritating dogs for a while, but it would be worth it to continue what was agreed between Rex and William to be a highly beneficial arrangement.

Four months later, the plan seemed to have gone off without a hitch.

Rex had selected a female Dalmatian from a nearby pound and introduced it to William in the kitchen. It had apparently been unhappy to be locked in there with William, who sustained one or two bites and scratches, but the noise of this meeting of dog and man-dog convinced Sylvia that a mating had been accomplished.

Months later the second part of the plan was put into action. Rex purchased a selection of the cutest puppies available and dumped them around the 'mother', who thankfully did not seem to mind too much. Again, the puppies seemed to find great sport in biting and scratching their reluctant 'father', but this only added to Sylvia's approval. Aside from the cacophony of howls, growls and whines that filled the house each day, Rex was satisfied that all was going according to plan.

Then, one Tuesday night, Rex crept downstairs for his regular conference with William. He wanted to discuss the feasibility of taking the pups to the pound along with the female adult. The economic downturn was making buyers hard to locate, and Rex was beginning to lose patience. He thought he could tell Sylvia that one Dalmatian fancier had turned up and given him a fortune for the job lot.

It would mean taking a hit in the pocket himself, handing over a phoney payment to his wife, but there was nothing to be done about that. He had been shaken by the return of genuine dogs to the house, and was resolved to be rid of them as soon as possible. Sylvia was becoming worryingly attached to them, and he thought speedy action was needed to prevent them from becoming permanent residents.

Rex entered the kitchen, expecting to be greeted by the usual odour of cigarette smoke and the sound of football commentary. Instead, he found the place empty. There was only a small piece of paper on the table, weighted down under William's collar. Rex picked it up and stared to read.

Rex mate,

Really sorry, but I'm out of here.

I bet you're asking why, when it was probably the most successful gig I ever had. Well, truth be told, my confidence in my ability has taken a bit of a knocking over the last few weeks.

> *She isn't interested in me anymore. Don't tell me you haven't noticed. She's obsessed with the bloody puppies. She's going to keep them, by the way—she's told me. That's about the last bit of news I've had out of her. She only talks to the pups now. Anyway, she never takes me for walks anymore, or scratches my belly, or gives me the Sir*

Lunchalot. She gives me the dry stuff from the corner shop instead.

Basically, she doesn't give me the attention that my character deserves, so I've taken another gig. There's this old dear living out in Croydon who's only got a tiny flat—no room for little ones—and I think my character would rather live with her than with someone who doesn't appreciate him. I'm a 'soul mate' kind of a hound, you see, not the dog that gets left to grow old by the fire while the puppies live the life. Dogs need love, you know. They crave it. Besides, these puppies are more 'real' than me, and if I'm honest, I feel outclassed—like some Hollywood type doing a cockney accent.

Anyway, have a look at Spotlight, and see who else is out there. You never know, there might be someone in rep who might like the challenge.

So long mate, and thanks for the chance you gave me.

P.S. I'm going to put this gig on my CV, if that's alright with you?

William

The next day, Sylvia couldn't get Rex out of bed.

He lay there sobbing with the pillow over his head, as the puppies and howled and woofed with the new morning.

She tried to comfort him, and said that she understood his pain, but that made him snap at her. He said that she could never understand. He said that she had made William run away. He said that she had done it deliberately because she'd never really liked William and was glad he was gone. He said that Sylvia had only ever wanted William for the puppies.

Sylvia decided to let him get his sleep, and whispered that she would take the puppies for a walk. She said that they could keep the puppies for longer if Rex liked, to cushion the blow of losing William.

Rex waved her away, dripping hot tears of loss onto the black collar he clutched in his hand.

Alex grew up in Australia but now lives in London. Like several contributors to this volume, her background is in film production, where she's worked for a variety of organisations including the BBC and the UK Film Council. 'The Puzzle' is her first published story.

The Puzzle

Alex Cameron

The old man sits in his chair, one shin crossed over the other; a leg slips out from beneath the towel of his dressing gown, revealing mottled, hairless skin, so taut it shines. To see his head lolling to one side on his chest, it would appear he is asleep but on closer inspection, beneath loose storks of grey hair heavy with grease, his eyes are wide open, glaring. Eyelids, pink and translucent, blink over murky green eyes—the colour of the Solent, toward which he stares. Rain begins to fall, big fat splotches, like bird droppings on his forehead: they have forgotten him again.

'Yoo hoo! Mr Valentine, Yoo hoo! You have a visitor,' calls the nurse.

Her voice, thin from guilt, quavers down the hill as he imagines her running. Her uniform, at first white against the green grass, begins to melt into her generous flesh, soaking with rain. Big Bertha.

'Oh, Mr Valentine, how silly of me. Sun'll be out in a sec, I bet. Still, better for a little fresh air for those squeaky lungs of yours.'

She straightens him up in the wheelchair, smothering his face with her chest, and slaps his feet back into place on the platforms.

The old man's bad arm falls out of the pocket of his gown and swings against the wheel of the chair. She picks it up and places it in his lap, while she jabbers about her colleagues and pushes him up the hill toward the sanatorium.

He's heard it all before.

On and on she goes, as if someone has permanently injected the wings of a mosquito into his head. To be able to open his mouth and scream at her to shut up is a luxury he does not have.

'...and that's when I arrived this morning to find you had a visitor. Yes, a visitor. Interesting man, he is. Dressed all in black. I said to myself, Bertha, what's his business coming here and wanting to see our Mr Valentine? Well, he was all mysterious, he was, Mr Valentine, wouldn't tell me a thing—wouldn't even open his mouth. Well, I warned him, of course, told him you wouldn't be able to speak to him, said you wouldn't understand him but it didn't matter a thing. Strange man indeed who wants to have a one-way conversation. Well, now, I think you can understand me, of course, Mr Valentine, but I wouldn't want you to become distressed like what happened that other time, and that's when I remembered Warren had put you out for the morning. Ah, now here we are. And what did I tell you, there he is, come out as I said he would—the sun.'

But there is no visitor, just a parcel wrapped in brown paper.

Mr Valentine's wheelchair is placed in the foyer, where the package rests on the reception desk. Shelley, the receptionist, sits on the other side of the bench. He cannot see her as the bench is chest height, but he imagines she is sipping from her mug that says, *Real women don't have hot flashes, they have power surges.*

'Where's that chap gone then, Shelley?' says Bertha.

'What chap?' says Shelley, over the impatient flutter of a magazine page.

'You know the one, here to see Mr Valentine, black shirt and trousers, bit of a snout on him?'

'Oh, yeah. Nah, he left, innit. Left that box there.'

Bertha dabs her face, chest and hair with a few tissues from Shelley's desk and then busies herself with his parcel. Water drips from his hair on to his lap; it sounds like the slap of a coin. Her flaccid cheeks, pink from the unnatural state of exercise, puff in and out as she wriggles her fingers beneath the brown wrapping.

'Oh, Mr Valentine, but there's no card. What a mystery!'

He hears the wrapping tear and sees it fall to the ground. Bertha picks up a plain cardboard box and shakes it.

Sounds like boxed rice, he thinks. No, something heavier: pieces of wood, perhaps.

Bertha looks at the old man. 'Ooh, what do you think it could be, now? I'll just go ahead and open this then, shall I?'

She lifts the lid, her eyes wide with expectancy.

'Oh,' she says. Then she bends down, bringing the box beneath his nose so he can see its contents. 'It's a puzzle.'

She places his good hand inside the box; he curls his fingers around one of the tiles as she wheels him through to the common room beside one of the card tables. Other guests sit on the blue vinyl chairs absorbing the low hum of daytime television. He is glad for a change; he finds the flicker of the TV hurt his eyes.

Bertha pours the contents of the box onto the table. The pieces clatter, a splatter of colours and shapes each of which she separates and turns face up. Then she grabs his wrist and places it, like a sock stuffed with sand, on top of the tiles.

'Well, that will entertain you for a very long time now, won't it?' She shuffles a few pieces around the board.

'Oh, there we go now. well, it looks like it might be...well...I can't for the life of me even begin to guess. Got to run now, it's time for elevenses.' He hears the whisper of her soft-heeled shoes departing for tea and shortbread with Shelley.

The old man sees she has made the beginning of a border. His fingers twitch on the table and his eyes blink, taking in the images before him. Rich pinks, reds and flesh colours swirl on the table; he can make out the faint scratches of a sable hair paintbrush. A painting. Judging by the colours and the tone it could be eighteenth century, a Delacroix, perhaps a Boucher, or the saucy flesh of a Rubens. He wills his arm to manoeuvre the pieces beneath him but manages only to scrape them along the surface, stuck on the underarm of his gown. He sees it then – a tile with the wisps of mouse-brown hair, a vacant eye welcoming the viewer and the pale skin of a model's face—the face of a neo-classicist heroine like those from *Le Salon de Paris*. Perhaps an Ingres? His preferred period. He didn't much care for the post-modern freestyle methodology that had become so popular during his lifetime. Where was the skill, the craftsmanship, the years of apprenticeship? Nowadays, it came too easily. That sort of art made him feel queasy.

'There you are, Mr Valentine. Enjoying your present? What a nice man to think of you. Perhaps he didn't quite know your condition. Well, lucky I'm here to help.' Bertha hums as she fusses around him, the nylon of her pantyhose zipping between her thighs as she pushes a chair up to the table and sits beside him with a mug in her hand that reads, *I may be fat but you're ugly, and I can diet.* She begins to fit a few more pieces together.

'Oh, Mr Valentine, it's a painting. I wonder what it is? You used to work with paintings, now didn't you? I bet you know what it is. Clever, you are, I'm sure. We heard you used to be quite a figure, selling art to all those rich people. Old Gracie, before she left, found a few articles on you, she did. Course, said we shouldn't mention anything, said there were a few things said about you after the war. But I said, "Gracie, what's past is past," and she just gave me one of her looks. Have to move forward, we do. Yes, Gracie's gone, she has. Oh, don't get me wrong now, Mr Valentine, I like old Gracie, I do, but goodness she could talk the hind leg of any animal, she could. Oh, there we go, she's one of them naked ladies from old times. I bet you seen a few of them in your time, didn't you, Mr Valentine?'

His fist clenches tighter around the piece of puzzle in his palm. To look at him carefully, the whites of his eyes would be larger than normal, strained against their pink rims, but the rest of him is motionless as if moulded in plastic. He hears something dripping again, thick this time, on to the tiles and feels a secretion, not unlike honey, ooze down his chin. His tongue, heavy and useless, lies limp from his distended lip. Bertha dabs his chin dry with the sleeve of his gown, before turning back to the puzzle.

'Us girls, you know, we've only known the country around us, born and raised on the tide of the river but you, from Paris. Marjorie went there once, said it changed her for life going up that Eiffel Tower. Mind you, she was always crawling up some tower or other. But you, Mr Valentine, the real thing—one who sold art. We didn't know the extent...well, shame you can't tell us what it was like, all those years in Paris. City of Lights, don't they call it?'

But his eyes are closed. Is this God's punishment? Does he deserve this? He never believed in God or Karma, just good old-fashioned money and hard work. And he had worked very hard— no one could have taken that away from him. They just took his body. A mind trapped in a lifeless body. Hadn't he been a good person? If he could raise his fist in the air he would have shaken it and sworn at the big man in the sky but all he could manage was a spasm that sent a few pieces of puzzle flying to the floor.

He'd worked so hard to keep the hunger at bay, to build up the cushions around him, never to want for anything again. Did it matter it was at the expense of others? As far as he was concerned it was every man for themselves. He'd seen enough violence and hatred to know that. But now, imprisoned in this lifeless body, waiting for his mind to go black—what did it all mean? He wished Bertha had left him in the garden, where at least he could feel the wind and the rain whiplash his skin, and his body shook involuntarily from the cold. Now what was he left with? Just bleeding memories, a life spent collecting and gathering, only to end up with nothing.

'Don't be exhausting yourself, Mr Valentine, you know your body still responds to stress. We don't want that, now do we? Remember last time?' She pats his leg and says, 'Perhaps it's time for your pills.'

The puzzle, he sees, is coming together. The naked toes of a woman peek out from a lush garden of roses and green vines, abruptly stopping short at her ankle where the picture is incomplete. Her foot tugs at his memory. He has seen so many paintings in his lifetime and has all but lost any emotional attachment to the art he has moved from one continent to the next, from one household to another, from the fingers of one dead person to those of the living.

Art had been a commodity for him, something he knew about. It was something he had traded to those who already had the wealth of food on their plates and yearned for beauty. He had only answered a service. Asked no questions and had expected no answers. He just did. Was there blood on his hands? The thought had never crossed his mind. It had been only an...opportunity.

Anyone who had felt the iron ache of an empty belly would have done the same.

'Here we go, luv. Open wide.' Bertha jerks his jaw open and shoves two fingers down his throat, prodding the pill down his passages. She follows it with a spurt of water, opening and closing his mouth. 'Down the hatch we go.'

He feels his throat gagging and his body tense. His hand clamps up, banging up and down on the table; tiles lurch into the air but the picture remains intact.

Bertha slaps his back, 'All over now.'

She tucks her uniform under her bottom and sits herself down, the air poofing out of the seat cover beneath her. The familiar clicking of her tongue, like the sound of a steam train.

A steam train.

A train on its way to Geneva with a crate full of canvasses, jostling against each other on a long journey to the new world.

The pills begin to take effect and he feels the warm ripple of calm through his body. His chest collapses slightly and his fingers relax over the tile in his palm. Bertha settles in to enjoy herself until it's time for the next meal: trays of cucumber sandwiches with their crusts removed, and candied custard for dessert.

It's dark when he opens his eyes. He blinks a couple of times to wash away the sleep and it is a few seconds before he realises he cannot stretch out and a moment before his memory floods back with the decaying smell of old people's flesh, to which he has never become accustomed. His chin and pyjama shirt are damp from constant drool. Sometimes he wishes he'd never made it this far, had given way to the hunger. Sometimes, when he dreams, he dreams of Them and all he can see are their shoes. Piles of discarded shoes in the rubble by the side of the road.

It is a moment before he hears Bertha's interminable cheery voice come to wheel him out for the evening's entertainment.

Two burly men in white shirts and trousers hoist him from the bed into his wheelchair. Here, he does not need shoes. Here, he wears socks. Polyester, itchy socks. For days he lives with a constant itch in his feet.

It's Thursday. Thursday means a visit from the local church choir; they will practice their Sunday performance and try to get the active ones to join in. It is run by the local church minister who wears his white collar and black shirt tight against his soft chest and leads a choir of mostly women, whose husbands have passed on in death and possibly in life. Each week they sing a selection of songs about goodwill and faith and each week he is wheeled to the front row where he has to endure their smiles and their pity, their waist-slung breasts jiggling underneath taupe cardigans. It is a long way from the dark halls of the Pigalle Club.

'Your favourite night, Mr Valentine,' Bertha says. 'Mildred's doing a solo from *Jesus Christ Superstar*. Here we go, and look I finished your puzzle. One piece missing, though, couldn't find it for the life of me. Well, I finished it anyway and oh my, she's beautiful. Might have seen her in one of those galleries in Paris, you might have, 'cause that's where I'd imagine she's kept. Bit racy o' course but we could always use a bit of that around here—liven things up a little, if you know what I mean. Lookee now at Mr Devonshire, he's just beaming tonight.'

Bertha wheels him to the front of the room where the minister sits at the piano tapping at the keys, face like a baby's bottom, and the women run through their scales in an upward curve of la's.

The old man has a sense of his body being more brittle than usual, caged in its skin. Both his good arm and dead arm sit tucked away, folded into his gown pockets. He tinkers the fingers on his good arm and begins to feel relieved. Still there, he thinks.

But Bertha does not see the alarm in the old man's eyes as he gazes at the complete puzzle, nor does she remember, in her haste to greet Mr Devonshire and take her place in the front row of the choir, to click shut the second brake. In her busy wake, she does not notice that one side of the chair has slid sideways against the table, leaving the old man unbalanced. As by now, Bertha has the minister gripped in a tight embrace, her décolletage crimson and her lips brimming like wet gills on a fish.

The old man's heart beats faster as he takes in the image before him. Two nineteenth century ladies recline, half-naked, a posy of flowers by their side and a gaping hole where the face of one should be. His mind ticks over in rhythm to the piano keys as Mildred opens up with the first notes of the song from *Jesus Christ Superstar*; her voice warbling on the high pitch as he is sent back to another time when he first saw this image.

He recalls the tingle he felt as he had held it in his hands, such beauty, such craftsmanship, over one hundred years old. He'd looked up at the man in front of him and asked where he'd got it.

'I'll worry about that,' he'd said. 'You worry about how much.' He'd nodded his head and turned the painting over, flinching when he saw the seal glued to the base, his fingers peeling away as if they'd been seared raw by poison. He'd turned it over again and let the beauty of the picture hang in the air. People did what they had to, he'd thought. He would just remove it; strip the small black seals from the back and no one would be any the wiser.

'If you can manage this one, there will be others,' the man had said.

A haunting moan comes from deep within his chest, which goes unnoticed by Bertha and the other nurses who by this time are clapping their hands along with the chorus.

His body rigid, he pushes with all his strength to move his good arm. For now he knows who brought this to him, knows that he has, at last, been found out. The pressure of the truth crushes his chest. Water clouds his eyes as his left side spasms and he fights to lift his arm toward the hole in the woman's face. But the movement only serves to fire his useless body into violent convulsions, jerking the wheels of his chair back and forth until he is propelled from his seat to the ground. He topples the table over in his fall and finds himself on the floor, the centre of a hundred pieces of puzzle.

Bertha sees this episode as if it is in slow motion. The choir stops still at the repetition of *Do you think you're what they say you are*. She rushes to his side, calling for the men in white, and sees his mouth gurn in grotesque seizures, as if he is trying to tell her something.

'What? What is it?' she says, but she knows he cannot speak.

His eyes will her to look at him but the whites turn back into his skull, his gums chewing away his cheeks.

'It's OK,' she says. 'We'll get you out of here.'

His body jolts involuntarily and his chest shakes, maybe in an attempt to siphon air.

Bertha crouches over him and looks into his staring eyes.

But there is no answer. The room is quiet and the old man now lies motionless.

She sits back on her heels, her face pale, and for the first time she is speechless. For there, nestled in the fleshy pillows of his palm, like a dead moth, is the missing piece to the puzzle. A woman's eye.

Matthew Licht is one of our American contributors, although he lives in Italy these days. He has an energetic, rolling style, which I think works particularly well in this story. For more of Matthew's stories, seek out his collection The Moose Show, *published by Salt.*

Dave Tough's Luck

Matthew Licht

Up on the screen was a kid with long curly hair and a weird squint, like a bug flew into his eye. He was playing drums, I mean *really* playing them, on a stage in front of an ocean of people, half a million, the biggest concert there ever was. He was in one of the hottest hippie bands, out of his mind on LSD, and he played so hard and hot, the sound reached off the psychedelic split screen, touched me with a burning stick and set me on fire.

So I had to learn to play the drums. I thought drums must be easier than instruments where notes come out.

More than twenty years later, sometimes I feel I haven't really got it yet. Sometimes I think I'm not even holding the sticks right.

First crummy kit cost me fifty dollars. Bought it from a hunchbacked former big band guy who finally threw in the sponge. His name was Munger, rhymes with 'from hunger', and he lived way the hell out in Queens. He led me down to his basement that stank of sweat and dust, and pulled a gray sheet off his drums. The blue glitter-flake shells and rusty rims looked like he'd personally chewed them with his big yellow square teeth. He got all hung up on the hi-hat cymbals, like he was throwing them in special, like he was doing me a huge favour giving me something that was supposed to be included in the deal anyway. He said they were a pair matched by Dave Tough.

At least old Munger from Hunger gave me the urge to hear what a drummer with a name as cool as Dave Tough sounded like.

I've still got those hi-hat cymbals. They sound perfect together, dark and sharp.

Got my initial chops courtesy of marching band practice. The maestro started me out on bass drum, so I learned to use my shoulders and elbows. Then he moved me up to the snare where it's all about wrists, fingers. I went to a giganto high school in Newark, so there were always plenty of games, parades, ROTC marches, block dances. Got tapped for a spot on the riser with a prog outfit called Zero. They were older guys who used weird time signatures, so I had to learn to count like a bastard. I also learned I wasn't the kid who took LSD and beat his soul out for half a million people at Woodstock. He went on to play prog crapola and fusion garbage. His life topped out at Woodstock, unless he wins the lottery twice or something. Maybe I should be glad I haven't topped out yet. There's still a chance it could happen.

Started giving lessons for a living when I hit thirty. Not many other gigs pay fifteen dollars an hour. I learned the hard way I can't handle office jobs, the whole steady life deal. Maybe playing drums does that to you. Or maybe it's the other way around. You're that way, so you play the drums.

Most people think monkeys can play the drums. Chimps got rhythm. Chain 'em down, hand 'em the sticks, they'll figure it out soon enough.

The Shrovers were a family that lived in a big house in Montclair. They stood out mainly because there were so many of them and because they had a lot of dough. They would come into Newark for symphony concerts, or the opera. They were a big family, seriously big on music. They'd all get dressed up in velvet, tartan and bowties. They could've crossed the river to New York for major-league performances, but they were civic minded. Maybe even patriotic, partisan, or provincial. The Newark Symphony was close to home so that's where they went.

Mr and Mrs Shrover occasionally got their pictures in the local papers. They made massive donations towards local culture, especially musical culture, which meant strictly classical. One time they got their picture in the paper, it was because Mrs gave live birth to triplets.

Brave pale smile on weary Mrs's face. Her black hair's cut mom-short. Paunchy Mr standing proud but freaked in the background. Three squished-looking kids sprawled across her lap. One of the three, Andy—*my* Andy—has one eye slightly open. He's the only one looking around, although he was the last one out. He came out a shade too late, poor little guy. But he was already squinting at the world. Just like the kid who took acid and set his drums on fire. Set me on fire, and I'm still burning, though nowhere near as bright.

The Shrovers were, as I said, a majorly musical family. They crowded around in the living room listening to Daddy Shrover's state-of-the-art hi-fi component system. They went to concerts as a gang. They all played. Daddy Shrover on oboe, Mama Shrover on piano and sometimes harp. The sexy Shrover sisters comprised a peewee string section. The older Shrover brothers played horns, like their pop. So naturally that's the direction the first two triplets took. Michael started tootling a silver flute practically before he could walk, and Matthew got his hand stuck in a French horn.

Andy was last. He hadn't got enough oxygen at some crucial point of the birth process. No oxygen equals no wind instrument. Andy was a retard, so Ma and Pa Shrover figured him for percussion. They must've seen the flyer I put up at Symphony Hall, trolling for timpanists with an itch to get hip.

The first time I saw Andy, he had a kooky smile stretched over his entire face. He stumble-ran over and jumped on me as I was being led, open-mouthed and staring, through the mansion's living room. Didn't know ceilings could reach that high, outside of basketball gyms. He held on like a drooling koala bear as Daddy Shrover explained, in the tone people use on retards, that I was going to be his teacher.

'Thee-thur.' Andy gurgled, and wiped his nose on the shirt I'd ironed half an hour previous.

We went out to the garage, a perfect place for orangutans to slam on garbage cans. I'd brought a rubber pad and a few pairs of sticks. I think Ma and Pa Shrover expected me to lug over a whole kit, a playground of drums and cymbals for slow little Andy.

Cello and viola fought a duel up in some bedroom or music room or home recording studio while I tried to get Andy to hold the sticks correctly. In other words, my way. But he had his own way of holding sticks. After half an hour, I let him have his way. What the hell. We started banging. The original plan was to teach Andy to count, if nothing else.

Andy already knew how to count. Maybe he couldn't say the words for numbers right, but he knew. He got a charge when I counted sixteenth notes: one-ee-andy, two-ee-andy, three-nee-andy. He thought sixteenth notes were all about him. Maybe they were. Maybe they are. Even with that weirdo grip of his, he had no problem with sixteenth notes, or thirty-second notes, or sixty-fourth notes.

Took me years before I could burn sixty-fourth notes convincingly.

Paradiddles made him slobber, but it was the slobber of pure joy. Paradiddles were nothing but fun for Andy. Ditto syncopation. If I played a figure, Andy could play it back. I said, 'Awright!' and rubbed his shoulder. He wanted a hug, and a shirt flap to wipe drool on.

Daddy Shrover almost patted my head when I checked out from beaming Andy's first lesson. He gave me a crisp twenty-dollar bill and waved away the five-dollar change I should've insisted on giving him. Hand the chimp an extra banana. Thanks, Bobo.

Back at my dump, I set up the muted practice kit I'd picked up at a music school bankruptcy auction. I unburied crumbling method books, including Dave Tough's *Advanced Paradiddle Exercises*, the only manual I really ever wanted, and finally found at a yard sale in Union. Bright blue cover shows skinny Dave Tough at the high point of his short career, set to pounce on what must've been an ultra-modern kit in those days. Practically put on white gloves when I used his book. Any notes I made went strictly in separate notebooks. I practiced full-on for over four hours that night. Hadn't gone four hours in years.

The Shrovers said they didn't mind if I took Andy to the basement in South Newark where me and the guys I played with did rehearsals twice or three times a week, depending on the gigs. The basement was where I kept my junk kit, an ancient silver-sparkle Slingerland that felt kind of like driving an old car that's barely holding together. Fun, but risky for a gig. Cracked cymbals, skins pitted with impact welts and half a hair from torn through, scorch marks from cigs left on the bass-drum shell. I had a handle-free spaghetti pot full of broken but still serviceable sticks on the floor. Looked like a porcupine cooking over a ghost fire. Break a stick or drop one, all you got to do is reach down. Drummers need the reassurance of infinite extra sticks. You get used to playing with different sizes in your hands, using the butts instead of the tips. Got to be versatile. Give me an axe handle and a washtub, I'll play them for you. I've got a whole slew of kits stashed around Newark, stacked in garages and basements near the most frequent gig venues. All bought off old losers who gave up. Never splurged on a custom kit.

Andy lit up when he took his first look at dull silver flake and lichen-splotchy brass. I plopped him down on a rug remnant, rolled up my sleeves to play my trademark solo. The master shows his disciple what he can do, on a good day.

Hot, down there in the basement. Caught a whiff of my funky sweat when I set Andy on the teetering swivel stool. See if I could get him to sit properly. In other words, upright, dignified, nothing moving but arms from the shoulder down, like the better black jazz guys. Nothing doing. Andy went deep into a slugger crouch and would not be budged. I could've gone at him with a cattle prod and it wouldn't have done any good.

Then Andy played my solo back for me. Paradiddles and reverse paradiddles. He even threw in some kick-drum triplets at no extra charge. Ever try doing a kick-drum triplet? They're hard.

Eventually I got my mouth closed again. My eyes shrank back to their normal size. What I had down there in the egg-carton-muffled, mattress- and rug-strewn basement wasn't just some robot drum machine, valid only in playback mode. I scratched behind Andy's ears, drew happy gurgles. I rubbed his skinny shoulders to see if he'd relax. 'Good stuff, Andy. Nice. Excellent. But now let's hear you play what's in your head.' Patted his head. 'Or your soul.' Rubbed his chest, like that's where the soul hangs out. 'Or your hands, your feet, your dick, wherever. Hear those drums, beating away? I want to hear them too. Don't worry about what you're gonna do. Just you and me down here. No one else listening. Don't think. Just go. Blaze. Burn.'

This, to a retarded kid.

But Andy didn't let loose with the inner drums. Maybe he didn't feel like playing his own stuff right then. Or maybe there was nothing there. He sat happy-faced on the stool like he was having a righteous time just holding chewed-up sticks and hoovering faded flaking drum-glitter dandruff into his green eyeballs and snot-crusted nostrils. Trickle of drool from the left corner of his mouth, like that drummer joke where drooling from only one corner means your stool's not on the level. Straighten yourself out. I wiped sweat off his face with my shirt.

One of the guys I played with, Lucky Joe, kept his junk guitar, a Danelectro lyre model with severely cracked paint, in the basement. I plugged into his torn-cone practice amp, hit a few chords. See if Andy picked up on how a simple rock or blues number works out. Nothing doing.

Swung the humming guitar behind my back, sat on the drum stool with Andy on my lap, moved his hands and feet for him like he was a drum marionette. 'Like this. Hi-hat and a little softer on the verse, ride cymbal and punch it on the chorus.' I counted one-ee-andy, two-ee-andy in his ear. He mewled and shivered in delight, but I was moving his hands, beating out the rhythm for him. Then I put the guitar down, sat Andy on the rug again and played a Gene Krupa syncopation as clean as twenty years on the instrument had gotten me. Handed Andy the sticks and switched places with him. Back came the Gene, with a cymbal flourish neither I nor the Great Kroop had put there. But it fit, perfectly.

That seemed to be how it worked, with Andy.

'Play that one again, Andy. You did good. But now do it over. Make it better, if you want.'

No reaction except he picked his nose, devoured the booger.

We switched places again. I closed my eyes and counted silently, breathed in time, internalized the beat for a Dave Tough triple-paradiddle figure that still stumps me occasionally. Dave

Tough was a real artist. His stuff seems simple, till you try to play it. Listen to his few scratchy records and the genuinely hard stuff sounds effortless, tossed out like he could do it whenever he felt like it. I nailed the trip-diddle shuffle, up to and including the cha-cha-cha and the flip-flop-fladdle finale. Andy nailed it right back at me, clean. Anything extra anybody might try to slap onto Dave Tough's demonic signature fills would be grotesque, indecent. Andy knew this instinctively, or some other way.

The basement suddenly felt disquieting, eerie. Solemnity seemed appropriate.

'Dave? Dave Tough? Mr Tough, is that you? Are you there? Have you come back in this form for a reason?'

No flicker crossed Andy's face. No knocking sounds, no lowered temperatures or bare light bulbs fading in and out. Séance mumbo-jumbo did not apply. Andy was only what he was, a retarded kid with some kind of bizarre gift. I was supposed to be teaching him drums, but he was already beyond me. All I had to do was figure out where the music inside him was, the rhythm, the beat, and get him to let it out, let me have it. That was all I had to do.

Mr and Mrs Shrover weren't exactly delighted when I told them Andy was a prodigy, a natural, basically Mozart with sticks, built-in metronome and a runny nose. What? Really? Better than our Alice, who plays the violin so sweetly the angels weep through their beatific smiles? Oh yeah. Better than that. But on drums. And then there's this problem I haven't been able to figure out yet.

The looks in their eyes projected visions of a slobbering gorilla chained to garish blue-red bongos in a cage at the back of the sideshow attached to a mangy-ass circus touring the Deep South. That was their unfortunate son's future, the way I'd spelled it out for them. Throw a quarter in the slot and the hidden jukebox plays a syncopated dance beat that snaps, crackles and pops. Andy the Rhythm Ape will play it back for you every time, right down to the cowbell hiccup.

'No, wait. Sorry. Maybe I'm giving you the wrong idea,' I said. 'I'm not exactly a verbal person.'

That wasn't the right phrasing. Not for people like the Shrovers.

'This stuff that Andy can play back...No, wait. He's not just copying. He throws his own stuff in. Like he's already got all his own chops. I mean, phrases. He throws stuff in where it fits, in exactly the right places, and it sounds great. What I'm trying to say is...this stuff he does, it's hard.'

Ma and Pa Shrover reluctantly trudged out to their mansionesque-in-its-own-right garage, where I'd left a psychedelic spin-art plastic practice pad on a tilted stand. Andy played back sixty-fourth note flares, press-roll buzzes and flams. He flawlessly repeated a triple-bounce Buddy Rich fill and a patented irresistible Tito Puente dance riff. But his parents didn't break out into spontaneous rumba. Andy dropped a stick, stopped cold. He stuck his hands down the back of his pants. Scratch 'n' sniff with his fuck-you finger.

Ma Shrover took Andy back to the big house for a snack, juice and a nap. Pa handed me the customary brand-new twenty-dollar bill.

'He imitates. He apes. Many children like Andy have that ability. The moment you try to join in with him, though, he stops. That's...that's not good, to put it non-verbally, for a prospective accompanist.'

'He's not just imitating. He tosses in...didn't you catch the triple-bounce paradiddle flourish? Mr Shrover, have you ever heard Dave Tough?' He looked like he was old enough to have caught the big bands of Woody Herman or Hank O'Hare.

'I have not.'

'Well, Dave Tough was...is...this, this real artist, a modern artist, on the drums. It's hard to explain. He made the whole thing sound new...He changed the way the drums get played. Changed the whole instrument, basically. I think Andy...'

'Your friend Tough...this Tough guy...is no doubt a good—a *real* good—drummer...'

'He died about thirty years ago, Mr Shrover.'

The image beamed from his eyes was of a zoot-suited bebop cat lying dead in a gutter with a needle sticking out of his arm.

I went on. 'I think Andy might be...'

'Then this Mr Tough of yours was, no doubt, a fine percussionist. Swell. He was also, presumably, a normal human being. That is to say, an adult person of normal intelligence, with good motor and social skills. Andy, through an accident of birth... avoidable perhaps, alas...will never be adult in that sense.'

'But...'

'We have consulted any number of specialists. We can only do our best to ensure that Andrew is comfortable, well provided-for and...happy. He seems happy with his drum lessons. But let's not fool ourselves. Let's not pretend it's music, please. We take music seriously, in our family.'

Busted back down to babysitter with sticks.

Lovely blonde Alice sent Mozart's notes floating our way as we walked back across the lawn. I felt hot, angry, but an extra forty dollars a week was more than I could sneeze at. I kept going back.

Without telling Andy's parents, I brought people down to the rehearsal basement to show them what Andy could do, so they could hear him. Wasn't like I charged admission. But everyone I brought down there was only amazed by the freak. Nobody could tell me what to do with Andy. Felt like I was the only one who knew what was burning inside him. The drums can burn you. Most people don't know that. Andy could burn me down, I thought, if he wanted to. Maybe I wanted him to dust me, even if I didn't know why. If I could only get him to do it. Teach him how.

Andy grew up. He turned into a hulking, healthy, gap-toothed kid with a fairly permanent boner drooling through his too-short corduroys. Mr and Mrs Shrover decided to send Andy to a special school down in South Carolina where there were plenty of other kids like him, boys and girls. The school featured a program called Musical Therapy. I guess none of the music therapy nurses or teachers or whatever they call themselves had an ear for what Andy could do. I got a mental picture of colour-coded xylophones, slobber-proof extra-large recorders. Special school workers don't want retards banging drums around them all day. Maybe I should've written or called to let them know they had a weird genius in their clutches, but I probably wouldn't have been able to express the concept properly to them, either. The non-verbal thing, you know. I'm a drummer. My job, basically, is to make people dance. I make them dance with my right foot. Backbeat gets people's hips pumping. The work's not steady and the bread's not too good, so I give lessons. I've had a few hot students. One of them makes a living from the drums. He goes out on tour. They call him in for recording sessions with big-name performers.

Andy graduated special school and came back to New Jersey. He lives in what they call a young adult community home. He's got a girlfriend, she's kind of cute. They both work at a supermarket, bagging groceries, stacking shelves, making pyramids with cans of corn. They like their jobs. They're happy. Andy remembers me, still calls me teacher. Still laughs like a nut when I turn a shopping cart into bongos or rub a couple of six-packs together and count out sixteenth notes. Sixteenth notes are still all about Andy. Only he doesn't play sixteenth notes any more. What for?

Sixteenth notes are for people like me.

American playwright and musician Jason Atkinson is making his fiction debut with this story. Like several of our contributors, he's lived abroad; and like several of our contributors, he's told stories in other media. On this evidence, I'd say that both are good training for writing fiction.

Assassination Scene

Jason Atkinson

'In the district we'll be seeing lower temperatures tonight. Highs in the 50s and rain in the afternoon.'

The radio emitted some variation of this every morning. His response to it was always the same: he hit the snooze button one time and then, upon the sounding of the second alarm, rose and began preparations. Clothes were already set out. Coffee programmed. Lunch packed. Before he became fully conscious, he was often already in the car. The engine hummed as he passed through the upper middle class suburbs.

Panera bread. Wal Mart. Costco. Arby's. Giant supermarket. He drove past them all before merging onto the highway. Many years ago he might have thought something negative about the ubiquity of all these franchises, but recently he had made his peace with them. They were here now, lording their wares over the good people of Vienna, Virginia. But they would pass, just as he would pass. Just as everything would pass.

It was better to enjoy their bounty, and try to extract something positive from the experience.

He took the Suitland Parkway into the District. Someone had once told him that the Suitland was on the National Register of Historic Places and he had to admit that, when fall came, it looked really beautiful. He always got a real good look at the beauty of the parkway because it was always full of traffic. The commuters move into the city. The commuters exit the city.

Despite years of doing this drive, he felt a surge of pride when the Washington Monument came into view. He felt powerful. Part of the power structure. Part of something big. Unprecedented. Important. Human beings were needed to make this government run, and he was happy to offer himself.

He caught sight of Capitol Hill. He was almost at the office.

He thought, 'I am in a car, and I am surrounded by other cars, and we are all driving towards a place where people wear suits. This is occurring on a parkway that is called The Suitland Parkway. The parkway is historical.'

He often felt this sounded like a fairy tale before the good stuff started. Government work was not a fairy tale. Government work was dull and confusing and filled with long corridors that went nowhere and offered no exit.

When he was younger, he'd wanted to get deeper inside. A beltway insider. Deep, deep inside. The centre. The centre of the centre. To the place where the man in the chair sat and said something and watched as his wishes were carried out.

He had not located this place. He had long abandoned his search for this place.

He settled. One has to settle. It would be a good retirement, he would receive a good pension, and then he would take what he could get from this life. It would involve sometimes being very quiet and very still and just listening to his heart beat and trying to get a sense of the blood being pushed through his body.

And then he, like all great nations, would pass away.

He parked and went into his office. He worked at the Federal Energy Commission. It was a good job. A government job means that you are set for life and, if you're not the greatest worker or the sharpest tack, or if you suddenly fade out, they won't just put you out on the street. They'll find a little corner for you in the complex mechanism and there you will sit until retirement.

He had his corner. He worked on issues that dealt with the United States power grid. It was a large and complex system. Vast and sprawling and impossibly powerful. It had been just an old boy's club for a long time, but when they screwed up in the NYC blackout, the government was finally able to get in there and regulate. And that is exactly what Daniel did. He regulated. It involved him writing down stuff on paper and examining things and correcting things and typing things into his BlackBerry. Sometimes something happened; most of the time it was just red tape and confusion.

As long as he checked and responded to his BlackBerry and did what the higher-ups asked (which involved late hours sometimes), he would be okay. They would let him retire and they wouldn't move him out of this office and into an even more godforsaken place. If he followed the rules, he would be safe here. Some days he wished that death would come and some days, especially when his kids were younger, he was grateful to have the peace of mind that a government job gave to a man.

He showed his big heavy plastic ID to guards at the door. He passed through the metal detectors. He greeted people he knew and turned on his BlackBerry at exactly the time he was expected to have it on.

He read the emails and found that he had to deal with something unpleasant today.

The new girl wasn't focused. She was young, hardly getting paid much of anything, and fresh out of law school. He had the unfortunate pleasure of telling her that she was not doing a particularly good job. If she didn't improve they would move her somewhere else. A different corner. An awful corner.

He contacted her and had her come into the office.

'You wanted to see me, Daniel?'

'Yes.'

She entered. She was kind of attractive. Not gorgeous or anything, but pretty attractive. She had on a pants suit and a set of pearls. She knew what she was supposed to wear and was a responsible human being. He wondered why she wasn't doing the appropriate things of late.

He let an appropriate moment pass.

'Sadie,' he said, 'we've been noticing that you've been a little distracted.'

Sadie looked frightened in the way a person gets when they are getting relocated to another department. But this wasn't that talk, this was the talk before that talk. Of course, she didn't know that.

'Is there something going on in your personal life?' he asked.

'Is my job in jeopardy?'

'No,' he said. 'But it could be if we don't modify some of your behaviours.'

'Am I not staying late enough?'

'Well, these past couple of weeks, a couple of the lawyers have noticed that you are first in and first out at the end of the day. There's nothing wrong with that, of course. But, if everyone is staying late, it probably means that you should stay later as well.'

'I know. I'm so sorry. I don't want to mess this up. I'll fix it.'

'It's okay.'

Daniel let some time pass. Experience had taught him that, in situations like these, it was better to stay quiet and let the other person talk.

'I over committed myself,' she said.

'Oh?'

'I agreed to direct a play.'

'I see,' Daniel said.

She began her explanation.

'I was, um, I have a friend and we were at Georgetown together and did a lot of plays. And then she had agreed to direct this play, but something came up for her in New York, and so I said I'd do it for her. I didn't realize what I was getting myself into.'

'Do you do this often?' he asked.

'No,' she said.

Daniel's BlackBerry buzzed. He ignored it.

'How many more rehearsals do you have?'

'About two more weeks' worth. But then there is tech. Tech is when they...'

'I know what tech is,' Daniel said. A harshness slipped out.

'Sorry,' she said. 'My job is my top priority. I'll quit the show, and I'll...'

'I used to do theatre when I first got to DC,' he said.

'You did?'

He had. Mostly stage managing. It was an incredible amount of work, and doing that plus law had been too much. This was at the very beginning of his time here in DC. Before the kids. When his energy was boundless.

'What play are you doing?' he asked her.

'Julius Caesar.'

'Great play,' he said. 'That has a lot of characters.'

'Too many,' she said.

Daniel smiled.

'But I'll call and let them know I can't do it,' said Sadie.

'No,' he said. 'You should do the play.'

'Pardon me?'

'Do it. I mean, let's find a way that you can do it. But it needs to be kept quiet. Don't mention it to the other associates.'

She was silent. They stared at each other for a long time. It occurred to Daniel that he was crossing an inappropriate line. He was being intimate with Sadie and taking her into his confidence. Could he trust her?

'Alright,' she said. She couldn't help but smile. 'But this work comes first for me. I don't want to...'

'This work is bullshit,' he said.

She got quiet.

'I mean, it's not bullshit. It's serious stuff. But it's...they don't need us. Anyone can do this. I mean, when we are gone and retired, it'll still be going. This whole machine will still be moving along. Life is about more than that. We should take these opportunities when they present themselves. Don't you think?'

Sadie nodded.

'I'm sorry,' he said. 'I shouldn't have said that. It's kind of a bleak way of looking at things.'

'That's okay,' she said.

Daniel felt that he should be activating Microsoft Word or pressing buttons on his BlackBerry.

'I think we can make this work for you. Of course, in the future, you should always make sure you schedule your extracurricular activities outside of crunch time.'

'Certainly, sir.'

'Anyway, if you need extra time during your tech, just come to me privately.' He said this in such a way as to indicate that she should be leaving. He was good at that.

'Okay.'

She got up. Then she turned and looked at him in a way he didn't like. It felt too familiar.

'Were you an actor?' she asked.

'I stage managed. I never acted.'

She was leaving and the words he had inside fell out of him. Against his better judgment.

'I'd like to do some acting, though. One of these days.'

She stopped at the door.

'Really?'

'Yes. I've. It's something I've always wanted to do. Perhaps when I retire.'

She stared at him for a moment, as if she was considering what to do.

'Well, we've got some small roles. Plebeians. Soldiers. Small parts. Some non-speaking roles. If you wanted to get your feet wet. There are a lot of roles to cast.'

He laughed. 'Are you offering me a role?'

'If you want one,' she said.

'I don't know,' he said. 'I'm not sure if I have time for that.'

Yesyesyesyes, he heard inside of himself. Acting would be fun. The words just kept repeating themselves over and over again, as if some unknown part of himself was insisting that he say yes despite his feeling that, for a workplace relationship with a subordinate, he was in incredibly inappropriate terrain.

'I might consider it, as long as the time commitment is minimal.'

'Okay,' she said. She was surprised. He could tell that she hadn't expected him to say yes. Was she just trying to be polite? The right thing to do in a moment like this would be to say something about how he was her boss and that it would be fun but probably inappropriate. But he didn't do that. He just let time pass. He stared at her.

'Okay. Do you want me to get the, uh, script? You could read for a part...'

'Are there a lot of lines?'

'Well, no. But it would help me to get a good idea of where to place you. Based on how you read the lines and all.'

'So I'd have to learn lines?'

'Maybe. I mean if you wanted to.'

He felt himself starting to get nervous. Maybe he should back out of this. It wasn't the public speaking that he would be uncomfortable with, so much as the memorization of the lines. Memorizing wasn't necessarily a big deal, but with Shakespeare... it was a big responsibility. Those were some of the greatest plays in the English language. They dealt with profound themes. It would be imperative that he enunciate and understand everything.

'Why don't you meet me at Potbelly over lunch,' he said. 'I'll buy. And we can quickly decide which part I'm going to do. Okay?'

'Okay.'

Then it was over and he was looking at his computer. Microsoft Word was open and he was reviewing a legal document that one of his underlings created a few days ago. It was filled with errors and inaccuracies. Little things that needed to be fine tuned before they could be released out into the government.

He worked through the errors and periodically stopped and checked his BlackBerry.

'Potbelly Sandwich Works' was an idiotic name for a sandwich shop. It made you feel fat and stupid, but it was better than eating at Subway. He got a turkey sub and chips. This retailed for almost eight dollars and this irked him too. He ate here, despite hating it, almost twice a week. He wanted something quick and convenient, but also good and memorable.

Sadie came in and sat down.

'Are you eating?' he said.

'I'm going to Chop't,' she said. 'I'm trying to eat healthy.'

'Chop't?'

'It's sort of like a mix and match salad place, around the corner. They started in New York City and I think they have stores in LA and Chicago.'

'Oh,' he said. He had not been to Chop't yet.

She smiled a young and beautiful smile. She was getting her first cheques now. Buying her first this and that. Learning how to save and spend money. Maybe she was planning her first nice vacation.

She took out a copy of the play and set it down on the table.

'Do you feel comfortable reading in the restaurant?' she said.

'Sure,' he said. He took the play in his hands. He saw the lines and the names of the actors. He remembered these Shakespeare editions from high school. They had the definitions of the archaic words on one side of the page and the play on the other. The occasional illustration.

'How about reading Flavius, the soldier from the beginning. It might be nice for you because he's just in the opening. You could come in, do your thing, and then go home for the night.'

He nodded. 'I do have a wife. I guess every night doing theatre is probably not such a good idea. Let's see...

'Hence! Home, you idle creatures, get you home!'

Tonight he would go home. Then he would be, as he always was, shocked at how little time he had to himself, despite the fact that all the kids were out of the house.

Sometimes in life you get the feel of time marching along. Sometimes it's jogging along. Sometimes it is so fast that you can't even see it. How have you used your time? Did you use it well? Did you waste it?

He finished reading the lines and looked up at her. She was looking at him. She looked confused. He felt a wave of embarrassment wash over him.

'I'm sorry. I have no business doing this, do I?'

'That was pretty good.' Sadie said.

'Good?'

'I didn't expect that.'

'Really?'

'Sure.'

'What was good about it?'

'You took your time. You stayed in the moment. It was almost like you were speaking to me.'

'That's good.'

'I'm getting older now. I guess you take things more slowly.'

'No,' she said. 'There are a lot of bad older actors. Believe me. We've been trying to cast Caesar, for instance, and it's been...'

She looked at him.

'Do you want to read for Caesar?' she asked.

'Caesar?'

'Our original Caesar just dropped out two days ago. I was going to ask this other person but...I don't know. If you'd like to read it, I think you might be able to do it.'

'Isn't that a serious role?'

'Would you take it if I offered it to you? I mean, I'd probably need to see you do one rehearsal with the cast, just to make sure you didn't tense up or anything.'

He shrugged.

'I can't believe you can't find someone to do Caesar.'

'I had a hard time finding people in that age range to do roles.'

'Really? Why?'

'I don't know. The ones that want to do it often aren't very convincing. The ones that can...I guess they're busy or something.'

'They have more important things to do than play Julius Caesar?'

She smiled again.

'Would you like to read it?'

He nodded. 'Why not.'

She opened up to a page. He read.

'Cowards die many times before their deaths;

The valiant never taste of death but once.

Of all the wonders that I yet have heard

It seems to me most strange that men should fear;

Seeing that death, a necessary end,

Will come when it will come.'

'Not bad,' she said. 'And you've only stage managed? You've never acted?'

'Never acted,' he said.

'Why don't you come to the rehearsal and give it a try. We're rehearsing the assassination tomorrow.'

'The assassination?'

'Yeah,' she laughed. 'Do you feel like getting stabbed by six people?'

He looked around Potbelly. He looked at the man making the sandwiches. He looked at the menu items. He watched the man behind the counter take the order, and he watched the customer wait for his order to be prepared. The soda fountains clicked off and on as people filled paper cups with sugary drink.

'I'll do it,' he said. 'Why the hell not.' And then she told him where they rehearsed.

That night, he drove home in a distracted state. Maybe this play thing was a bad idea. It was tiring to do plays all day and then go home, get up, go to work, and then tack on a rehearsal. His exercise regimen would be disrupted. He would start eating poorly. His wife, with whom he hadn't really had a conversation in the past two months, would get irritated.

He and his wife had developed, after twenty years of marriage, a very strange relationship. She had her house to maintain, and her friends, and the garden to plant and maintain, and the quiet resentment of giving up career for children. It was all very stressful for her and, when they talked for too long, he would be reminded of the extent of that stress despite the fact that, when she had been working, she had hated her job.

It was better to just not talk. Dinner, now that the kids were out of the house, usually consisted of something really simple. He would eat a salad with grilled chicken or go and buy sushi from the Giant. Sometimes he would wander over to the frozen food aisles and buy some organic frozen dinner that seemed healthy. He would arrive home and just eat it in front of the TV. At first, when the kids moved out, it was kind of fun.

Briefly, they reformed. They tried to eat together. They strained for things to talk about and mostly just sat in silence. Everything had been discussed. Everything except the immediate concerns of the evening: what to eat, what to drink, what time to go to bed.

'I already ate a little something,' she said, and then he was back in front of the TV. Some marriages were probably more exciting, he guessed.

Time passes.

'I'm going to bed,' she said at some point.

'Goodnight.'

'There is some stuff in the fridge that's going to go bad. You should bring it for lunch tomorrow.'

'Okay.'

'I'm going to work late tomorrow.'

'Alright.'

He didn't mention the play. He would tell her, though. She might even like it.

The next day was blurry. He did his job. It was an autopilot day. He kept looking at Caesar's words. The words of a statesman. A powerful man says things that the rest do not say. He stands apart.

Caesar was the man at the centre. The man who stated his wishes and let them be carried out.

And then the knives slipped inside.

He took Metro to get to the rehearsal. He hadn't been on Metro in fifteen years. If you have a car and you live in the suburbs it just doesn't make sense to worry with Metro. Things are just too spaced out. But he loved Metro. He remembered when he was over at Georgetown in the eighties and when they first put in the stations near them. There was excitement. The stations felt like something out of a science fiction film or some sort of strange German opera that lasted five or six hours. When his parents came to visit they would marvel at the weird architecture. They would just marvel at it.

'Welcome to Washington, DC,' he would say. He had pride in his city.

Nowadays, the Metro was fading. It was getting old. Its progressive design looked dated and cold. Bureaucratic.

'Welcome,' Sadie said.

The rehearsal was in a little black box at a community centre in a part of town that had become cool in the past five years. Everything was a bit dingy and run down, and the first thing he thought was that he was definitely not going to be inviting any of his friends from Vienna out here for this show. The age range was mixed. All white people. A couple of young people. A couple of older people. Folks, like him, still in business suits and ties.

A man came up to him.

'I'm Bill. Fight Choreographer. Are you the new Caesar?'

'I guess so,' he said. Just saying that made him feel pretty good.

'Ever been stabbed before?'

'I cut myself once chopping onions.' That was his attempt at a joke.

Bill laughed and brandished a dull stage knife. He pointed to the cast. Each held a knife.

'Everyone, this is Daniel,' said Sadie. 'He might be playing Caesar.'

He wasn't Caesar yet.

'Nice to meet you,' they all said.

'Bill's gotta run,' said Sadie. 'So we want to rehearse the stabbing scene really quick. Okay?'

'Sure,' said Daniel.

The fight choreographer started into his speech.

'Okay,' Bill said. 'I want you to imagine one of these blades going inside of you. Think about these blades. They're gonna hurt. First cut is gonna be in your leg. Femoral artery. Already, that wound is gonna kill you. That's gonna knock you back, y'know. You're gonna be stumbling around. Next cut is coming in from the other side. Now he's gonna flow up with a stab into your side. That's gonna puncture a lung and you're gonna have trouble breathing. Once that's done, someone's gonna come over here and get the other lung, and then someone's gonna get you right in the back. RAM it into your back. Follow me?'

Daniel nodded.

'You can't breathe. Blood is pouring out of your mouth and then you stumble over to Brutus and he'll slit your throat. Already you're going numb, but your brain is able to register your throat opening up. When that happens, provided the cut is deep enough, the blood is just gonna gush out. Gonna go all over the place. You'll just be barely conscious enough to feel this.'

'Wow,' Daniel said.

'Questions?' Bill said.

'How long will it take me to die after they cut my throat?'

'Well, once the throat cut happens you are pretty much completely numb. You drop like a stone, but, in order for you not to get hurt, we'll have Brutus bring you down gently.'

'Who is playing Brutus?'

'Here.'

He turned. Brutus, who looked to be in his early thirties, nodded. He was wearing a suit and tie. They shook hands.

'I'm Albert,' he said.

'Nice to meet you.'

'Do you work on the hill?' Albert asked.

'FEC.'

'Department of Labor,' said Albert. 'You look like you'll make a good Caesar.'

'Thanks.'

'Okay,' the fight choreographer said. 'Let's give it a try. This will be just a quick run through, and then we'll work it out in more detail.'

They positioned him.

'Speak, hands, for me!' yelled one of the actors.

Before he knew it he felt the dull knives on his flesh. One from the side and then one from the back. Someone pulled back his jacket. One from the front. Another one from the back. A push forward. He fell down on his knees. He tried to imagine what it would feel like to have all that metal shoved inside of him. He tried to get a sense of what the feeling of death might be like with all of that blood pouring out of him.

He coughed and spluttered.

'Good,' Sadie said. 'Now stand up and go to Brutus.'

He was playing. He knew this wasn't real. It felt stupid. Yet something compelled him on. Compelled him to drop down and to try to act like he was dying and stand up now and stumble over to Brutus.

'Et tu, Brute?' he mumbled.

Brutus matched his gaze and, after a long moment, slowly ran the knife across his throat. Daniel tried to imagine the flesh of his throat parting and the blood flow running down his clothes. It would drench him and he would slowly fade away.

'Then fall, Caesar.'

As he was lowered he imagined everything falling into darkness and passing away.

This was the beginning of the fairy tale, he thought. The part where the man on the parkway begins his adventure. He thought all this while knowing that it wasn't true. But it kind of felt true right now. And that was enough.

The last thing he heard as Brutus set him down on the floor was the voice of Sadie.

'I think we have a Caesar.'

He stood up and felt like he could probably die all night.

Back in 2009, Patrick Whittaker won the British Fantasy Society's short story competition with 'Dead Astronauts', about a man who keeps finding dead astronauts in his garden. It's a nicely handled slice of the absurd, as is this new story.

Celia and Harold

Patrick Whittaker

It was St Valentine's Day and I'd been on the train for five hours. My senses were numb, my throat was parched, and the reports I'd been immersed in since leaving London threatened to induce a coma.

As the train rolled into Midwick, I closed my laptop and put on my raincoat.

It was a dull little town, built on the sides of a valley and cut in two by the railway and a river. Terraced houses ribboned the streets. Next to the station, an abandoned linen mill sat like a carcass with its bones picked bare.

The guard wasn't happy about stopping in Midwick. 'We usually roll right on through,' he declared. 'Never any reason to stop.'

'I have to get to Nether Willows,' I told him. Normally that would have involved a change at Gilton Minor but the station there was closed for repairs. Going via Midwick added hours to my journey but I had no choice.

No one else got off and the train rolled on just as soon as it could.

Grey drizzle, so fine as to be barely more than mist, greeted me.

I checked my watch against the station clock. The timepieces agreed I had two hours and seven minutes until my next connection. Time enough for a leisurely lunch.

In lieu of a buffet, the station boasted a windowless waiting room with a coffee machine and a wooden bench. I decided to find a pub.

The first thing I noticed was the barfly perched on his stool. He was hunched over the bar, beer in one hand, chin resting on the other. All the gloom in that dingy room seemed to emanate from him.

The landlord stood on the other side of the bar, drying a pint glass. He was a stout fellow with a ruddy face and mutton-chop sideburns. There was no one else in the pub, but that suited me just fine. I was after a drink, not company. So why I sat on the stool next to the barfly, I'll never know.

As the landlord poured me a pint of Pudfrugger, my body language made it plain I wasn't one of life's listeners. Some men keep their sorrows to themselves, but the barfly didn't look the sort. And I wasn't about to give him reason to think he could unburden his soul on me.

After handing me my change, the landlord retreated to his back room, leaving me alone with old misery guts. I looked around at all the empty tables and unoccupied chairs. Over by the window was the least gloomy spot. Through the rain-drizzled glass, I would have a fine view of the tenements and alleyways of Midwick.

But the barfly made his move before I could make mine. 'You've not seen her,' he said. 'Pray you never do.'

'You'll have to excuse me,' I said, patting my laptop and nodding in the direction of the window. 'I have to get this work done before the train to Dymthrop arrives.'

The barfly snorted. 'Forget Dymthrop. All that matters is that you get out of Midwick—and fast. Or you'll be as doomed as the rest of us.'

He turned towards me and I saw the circular scar below his eye. It was about a centimetre in diameter and looked angry and fresh.

'Take a good look,' he said. 'Get used to this face. Because unless you're luckier than me, you're going to be spending an awful lot of time with it.'

It sounded like a threat. The fact I didn't understand what he was talking about made it no less menacing.

I looked at my watch. 'Dear lord! I hadn't realised the time. I have to be going, or I'll miss my train.'

As I headed for the door, the barfly called after me. 'That's it! Run, mister. And keep on running till you can't run no more.'

The rain was distilled essence of Midwick: grey, grim and oppressive.

Head down, laptop tucked beneath my coat, I hurried towards the station. Roadside gutters guided rain and litter into the sewers. I jumped over a child's tricycle.

With each step I took, the barfly's advice to get out of Midwick sounded more and more sage. Everything about the town seemed designed to grind a man's soul to dust.

Get the next train, I told myself. Go anywhere.

A man stepped out of an alleyway. I stopped suddenly to keep from ploughing into him.

It was the barfly. He must have taken a shortcut from the pub.

'Go away,' I told him. 'I don't want to know.'

He stepped meekly aside and let me hurry on.

When I got to the station, there he was again. Standing on the platform, a plastic cup in his hand. He blew on the cup's contents, causing a small cloud of steam to rise and dissipate.

Pretending not to see him, I turned my attention to the destination board. The next train was in an hour. It wasn't going to Dymthrop but it would get me out of Midwick.

On the way to the pub, I'd noticed a small café. Tea and bacon sandwiches would see me through the next hour. And if the barfly bothered me there, I'd have a word with the owner.

Outside the station, I looked back and saw the barfly still on the platform, still with a cup in his hands. But when I entered the café, he was at a table with a mug of tea in front of him.

He gave me the briefest of glances before taking out a hip flask and tipping some of its contents down his throat. The scar on his face seemed to grow angrier.

There was no one else in the café. Selecting a table as far from the barfly as possible, I sat facing his back and waited to be served.

From his coat pocket, the barfly produced a pink envelope decorated with a glitter star. He opened it and took out a card which he stood on the table. The front of the card showed a teddy bear holding a red rose. *Be My Valentine*, said the slogan.

'Bloody women,' he uttered. His shoulders heaved up and down. He let out a sob and cried, 'Why, Celia? Why?'

That was it. I wasn't going to sit around watching a grown man wallow in abject self-pity. Especially not on St Valentine's Day.

I took my laptop and went.

Returning to the pub, I was only mildly surprised to find the barfly back in position on his stool.

My initial inclination was to about face and find some place else. But the barfly knew this town and all its short-cuts. If he was determined to dog me, there was little I could do about it.

My only sensible course seemed to be to ignore the fellow. I certainly wasn't going to let him drive me out of the pub a second time.

The landlord was over by the fireplace, polishing a brass horse. 'Be with you in a second, sir,' he said without turning around.

I stood at the end of the bar and wondered what was coming next. There was something not right about Midwick, something beyond the fact that one of its inhabitants was stalking me.

The sound of a door being opened caught my attention. When I saw the barfly's twin emerge from the toilet, things suddenly made an annoying kind of sense. I hadn't been bumping into the same man! There were two of them, each with the same features and the same clothes. They'd even gone so far as to sport the same damned scar.

But why put all that effort into playing a practical joke on a stranger? Wasn't there anything better to do in Midwick?

The twin sat on the stool next to the barfly and took out a pink envelope with a glitter star. 'I suppose you got one of these,' he said, dropping the envelope on the bar.

'I tore it up,' said the barfly.

'She's a cow, isn't she?'

'A bitch. Evil through and through.'

'When I saw she'd sent me a valentine card, I thought she was trying to make peace. That maybe she wanted to talk things through.'

'Yeah. Same here.'

'Did yours have the poem?'

'Roses are red. Violets are blue. Verrucas aren't wanted. And neither are you.'

'She didn't use to be so vicious.'

'She's not the girl she was when I first met her.'

'That's for sure.'

The barfly knocked back the remains of his beer. 'Tell you what, Henry. I've some whisky back at my place. What say we go get drunk?'

'Sounds good to me, Henry.'

As the twins headed for the door, the landlord arrived behind the bar. 'Sorry to keep you waiting. What will it be, sir?'

'A pint,' I replied. 'And a packet of crisps.'

'Right you are.' The landlord set about pouring me a pint of beer. 'You staying in town long?'

'No longer than I have to.'

'Very wise, sir. Very wise.'

I took my beer and crisps over to the window table. The rain had stopped and a break in the clouds allowed the sun to bless Midwick with a modest amount of sunshine.

As I sat down, I saw a car go by. I could have sworn it was driven by the barfly or his twin.

I fired up my laptop, opened my crisps and swigged some beer.

Across the road, a front door opened. The barfly stepped out and hurried off down the hill. A moment later, he came out of the house next door and headed in the opposite direction.

Just as he disappeared from view, he walked into the pub.

So there were three of them! Identical triplets on a mission to take the rise out of strangers.

'Afternoon, Henry,' said the landlord. 'Haven't seen you for a while.'

Oh, ha bloody ha, I thought.

'I've been teaching myself to meditate,' said Henry, propping himself on the bar with his elbows. 'I'm trying to regain my inner peace.'

'Is it working?'

'I thought so. Until this morning.' Henry produced yet another heart-adorned envelope. 'Found this on my door mat. The bitch just won't leave me alone.'

'Looks like you've all got one.' The landlord pointed to the envelope recently deposited on his bar.

'Why can't she let us be?'

'Try to move on, Henry. Forget about her.'

'How can I, Charlie? Everything I do or see reminds me of her. I'm never going to get her out of my head. Never!'

I took a handful of crisps and crunched them loudly to block out the conversation. The beer was warm and malty, just the way I like it.

Wanting to distract myself, I turned to my laptop and delved into sales reports, profit projections and product specs. I was vaguely aware of others entering the pub, of drinks being ordered, of conversations building up and petering out. But I paid no heed to my surroundings. Until my beer ran out.

Clutching my empty glass, I started towards the bar and took two steps before stopping dead in my tracks.

There were about twenty other people in the pub. Three were propping up the bar; the rest sat in small groups. And all of them were identical.

That was it. I'd had enough of Midwick and its strange inhabitants. I was getting the hell out.

As I approached the station, I could see someone standing on the platform. Whether it was the same person as before, I had no way of telling.

I checked my watch. The next train was due in twenty minutes.

For a brief moment, I considered waiting outside the station. But I didn't want to run the risk—no matter how small—of missing the train. Come hell or high water, I was going to be on it when it rolled out of Midwick. And in the meantime, if the guy on the platform tried anything, he'd get a taste of my fist. But I needn't have worried. When I got to the platform, the guy was standing at its edge, clutching a pink envelope and crying. So wrapped up was he in misery, he remained unaware of my presence.

I bought myself a cup of coffee from the machine in the waiting room. It tasted of cardboard and chicory. Through the doorway, I watched the Midwickian tear up his valentine card and throw the pieces onto the track.

I turned my back on him and told myself it was time to find a new job. One that didn't involve spending time in towns like Midwick.

As I finished my coffee, I heard a train approach. With a sense of relief bordering on euphoria, I tossed my cup in the bin and hurried outside. The man on the platform had replaced his valentine card with a photograph. He held it before him like a hymn book.

I heard him moan. 'Oh Celia!' he cried. 'Why, Celia? Why?'

The train's whistle blew to announce it wasn't stopping. My own train wasn't due for another five minutes. I stepped back. The man with the photograph stepped forward.

He connected with the front of the train before he'd even hit the ground.

The driver slammed on his brakes. By the time the train came to a halt, its locomotive and front two carriages were already beyond the station. Numb with shock, I watched the driver climb from his cab and look beneath the carriages for a shattered body. On the train, faces stared out at me. They had no way of knowing why they had stopped. Their expressions spoke only of mild curiosity and boredom.

The train guard let himself out of the rear carriage. He called down to the driver. 'What is it, Bob?'

The driver made a cutting notion across his throat and the train guard paled.

'Crap,' he muttered. 'That's the third one this week.'

The rail men converged on the spot where the Midwickian had jumped. They crouched down to examine the body.

'There was nothing I could do,' pleaded the driver. 'It wasn't my fault.'

'I know,' said the guard soothingly. 'It's this town. They're all crazy here.'

Behind them, the dead man's photograph floated on a puddle of dirty water. It was a head-and-shoulders shot of a ginger-haired woman. So now I knew what Celia looked like. Incongruously, I thought to myself that she was no great beauty. And then I remembered a man had just killed himself over her.

I should have stuck around. Waited for the police to arrive and take my statement. But it would have delayed my departure from Midwick by quite some time, and that just wasn't going to happen.

The destination board delivered the inevitable news that the next train was cancelled—presumably because of the events I had just seen unfold. So it looked like I would have to wait for the Nether Willows train after all.

I had no desire to return to either the pub or the café and there was precious little else on the south side of town. So I decided to cross the river and check out the other side. Perhaps there I'd find a pub that wasn't full of crazies.

Outside the station, a footbridge spanned the railway and the river. It looked like the only way to get across. I'd just set foot on the first step when a hand grabbed my shoulder and a voice said, 'Don't!'

Shrugging off the hand, I turned around. And there he was again. Same face. Same clothes. Same scar beneath his eye.

'Keep away from me,' I warned, raising my laptop. 'I don't know what you're all playing at here but a man's dead because of it.'

'Several actually. Midwick is fast becoming the suicide capital of England.' He placed himself between me and the bridge. 'You need to leave Midwick now. Before it's too late.'

'Get out of my way!'

'Don't cross the bridge. I'm begging you.'

'Move it!'

'No!'

It was a flash of anger. Even as my laptop struck his head, I found myself thinking: Don't do it! But I couldn't stop myself.

For a sickening moment, I thought I'd split his skull. But it was the laptop's case that had cracked. Nonetheless, there was blood.

The man sat on the footbridge steps, one hand over his wound. He looked up with the most haunted, pitiful look I had ever seen. 'I was only trying to help,' he said. 'Trying to save you.'

'I'm sorry.' I felt wretched. 'I don't know what came over me.'

'It's not your fault. It's Celia. She drives men crazy.'

'Let me get you to a doctor. That wound needs looking at.'

'No need. I've had worse. I used to play rugby for England.'

I wondered if he was having a joke. He didn't look like a rugby player. In fact there was nothing about him to suggest any sort of sporting prowess. Besides which, I followed both codes of rugby and his face rang no bells.

Taking his hand away from his wound, he rubbed at his scar. There was less blood on his scalp than I'd feared, and it seemed well on its way to clotting.

'What club did you play for?' I asked.

'Saracens.' A rugby union club. 'That was before I became Henry Mason.'

Guilt made me want to humour him. 'So who were you before?'

'Lee Chesterton.' He smiled. 'Not that I expect you to believe me.'

'Listen,' I said, not believing him. 'If you won't let me take you to a doctor, at least let me buy you a drink.'

'Only if you're willing to listen to how I and just about every other man in Midwick came to be Henry Mason.'

'You've got a deal, Henry. Or is it Lee?'

'Call me Henry. Everyone else does.'

And so I found myself back in the pub. In a room full of Henry Masons, all competing to be the most dejected person on the planet.

The table by the window was unoccupied and I suggested to Henry that he grab it while I got the drinks in. But he vetoed the idea, saying he preferred not to see outside in case a certain lady came strolling by.

After nearly taking our pints to the wrong Henry, I located the correct one at the table furthest from the window. He was dabbing at his hair with a damp tea towel, removing the worst of the congealed blood.

We each demolished half our beer before he began the story of Henry Mason and Celia Cartwright.

Having both grown up in Midwick, they'd vaguely known each other all their lives but were never on more than nodding terms. That is until they found themselves sitting next to each other at the church bingo. They got talking and found they had a lot in common. One thing led to another and they became an item.

'At first everything was great,' said Henry. 'We made each other happy, had fantastic sex, laughed at each other's jokes, finished each other's sentences. Blinded by love, I couldn't see

Celia's many faults, and was convinced I'd finally found the right woman for me.

'The first squabbles were minor. I saw them as lovers' tiffs and took them as a sign that our relationship was on solid footing. But each spat was slightly worse than the last, and it wasn't long before we were throwing things at each other.

'I'd like to say some of it was my fault, but it wasn't. Celia Cartwright was—and is—neurotic and insecure. Paranoid too.

'At the beginning, I tried to placate her. The word sorry was forever springing from my lips. But after a while, I got fed up with being her doormat and started standing up for myself. And that's when things got really bad. My answering back was petrol to her fire.

'Sometimes we'd be up half the night screaming and shouting. We said the vilest, nastiest things imaginable. Made threats. Sometimes even came to blows.

'It's a wonder we didn't kill each other.'

'Vicious she was,' said another Henry on his way to the toilet. 'Tell him about the scar.'

My Henry pointed to his face. 'You see this? She did that with her cigarette. Tried to stab me in the eye. I'm lucky not to have been blinded. And that's when I decided enough was enough and told her it was all over. Without a single word of comfort or regret, she just upped and left.' He slumped. His already weary expression became wearier still. 'About a week later she rang and begged me to take her back. And I said no, even though it broke my heart. Truth is, I still loved her and I will until the day I die. But I knew if we ever got back together, one of us would kill the other.

'Oh, you should have heard her weep and beg and threaten. It was pitiable. She said she couldn't get me out of her mind. That every man she saw looked like me.

'After all that, I had to have a drink. So I came to this pub, only to find I was already here, sitting at the bar with a large scotch in my hand.

'Now this is the funny thing. I'm telling this story as if I've always been Henry Mason and that's not the case.

'Back when I was Lee Chesterton, I didn't know Celia or Henry. Until one day I was walking along, minding my own business, and a woman leapt out of a shop doorway. She was wild-eyed and wore a grubby shell suit with holes in the elbows.

'I thought she was some bag lady who'd maybe had too much white cider. As you do in such situations, I kept my head down and tried to hurry past. But she threw herself to the pavement and grabbed my legs, rendering me immobile.

'"Oh Henry!" she cried. "Why did you ever leave me?"

'And I looked down and saw not some drunken bag lady, but my Celia. She was in need of a wash, but still as fragrant as ever.

'Even before I saw my reflection in the shop window, I knew I was Henry Mason and I remembered her words on the telephone. About how every man she set eyes upon looked like me.

'Horrified, I pushed her away. She lay in the gutter weeping and moaning.

'As I ran back towards the bridge, I saw her again and again. She was in the newsagents. She was in a back garden hanging out her washing. She was simultaneously going into and coming out of a pub. She was everywhere!

'A rational person would say I was projecting. That none of the women were Celia. But they were! I knew the very act of my seeing them as Celia made them so.'

I shook my head. 'But how is it possible?'

'It's the power of love. They say our perceptions shape reality. Maybe this kind of thing happens more than we think. Or maybe Celia is the devil incarnate.'

I had to get out of Midwick. Before a Celia Cartwright saw me. Before I became another Henry Mason in a town full of them.

From the Henry who used to be Lee Chesterton I learned there was no bus service through Midwick. He advised me to walk along the valley to Nether Willows, the next town along.

'What about a taxi?' I asked.

'The drivers daren't leave the village,' said Henry. 'None of us do.'

'Because of Celia?'

'Every time a Henry Mason sees a woman, she becomes Celia. And when one of those Celias sees a man—pouff!—another Henry.

'If any of us left Midwick, the consequences would be catastrophic. In next to no time, there'd be a plague of Henrys and Celias. We're a chain reaction waiting to go off.'

A thought occurred to me. 'Why haven't I seen any of these Celias?'

'We can't live with her; we can't live without her. But for the sake of peace, all the Henrys live on this side of the valley and all the Celias live on the other. Now do you see why I stopped you crossing the bridge? You wouldn't have lasted two minutes before becoming a Henry.'

I shuddered at the narrowness of my escape. 'Let me buy you another drink, and then I'll be on my way to Nether Willows.'

'Now you're being sensible. Once you're out of this nightmare, don't look back. Just keep on walking.'

'Oh, I will,' I said. 'I will.'

Two dozen mobile phones went off at once. Two dozen Henry Masons answered them.

'Henry Mason,' they cho:used. Then, after a short pause: 'Celia! What the blazes do you want?'

After that, each Henry reacted to his Celia in his own way. Some swore; some cried. Others threatened. A few hung up almost immediately.

My Henry grabbed my arm. 'You've got to go. Now!'

Another Henry looked out the door towards the other side of the valley. 'My God! She's not kidding!' he bellowed. 'They're marching towards the bridge! They're on their way.'

'Get out!' said my Henry. 'Go out the back way and up the hill. You'll find a path at the top that will take you to Nether Willows. Remember, if any Celia so much as gets a glimpse of you, you're done for.'

'What's happening?' I asked.

'The Celias have declared war. They say if they can't have us, nobody can.'

As the Henrys set about barricading the pub, I snuck out the back. Ten minutes later, I was on the path at the top of the valley.

Behind me, I heard the sounds of a pitched battle.

The path ran gently downhill and took me through woodland. After about an hour, I found myself back at the bottom of the valley and on the road to Nether Willows.

My legs ached. I wasn't used to this kind of walking and my shoes were made for offices, not hills. Things were made worse by my laptop, which seemed to weigh ten times as much as when I'd left Midwick. I didn't even know if it still worked.

I was beginning to doubt I would ever make it to Nether Willows, when I heard an engine.

Standing at the side of the road, I saw a battered Renault coming up behind me. Judging from its rattle and the smoke billowing in its wake, it was in need of a mechanic's loving attention, but I didn't care. It was as welcome to me as a lifebelt to a drowning sailor.

I stuck out my thumb and silently promised God that if the car stopped I would do all sorts of nice things on his behalf.

With a teeth-curling crunch of gears, the car slowed and came to a stop. The driver pushed open the passenger door and yelled, 'Get in! Quick!'

I hurriedly complied.

It was only as I settled into the lumpy passenger seat that I realised my laptop was gone and my clothes had changed.

Then I looked at the driver and my heart gave a beat. It was Celia. Dear, sweet neurotic Celia in her distressed shell suit, looking as beautiful as ever.

'It's up to you, Henry,' she said. 'We can go back to Midwick and get killed with the rest of them, or we can get the hell out and begin again.'

The scar beneath my eye itched, indicating it was on the mend. I took it as a good sign.

Charles Lambert has published two novels, Little Monsters
and Any Human Face, *and a collection of short stories,* The
Scent of Cinnamon. *Something that always stands out for me
in his work is the way he breathes life into his characters.*

All I Want

Charles Lambert

He's strolling out of Teddy's classroom when I first spot him,
carrying a briefcase and a folded newspaper. Most students are
in shirtsleeves, light summer dresses, but this man's wearing a
sharply tailored dark suit, white shirt, a slim red tie. His hair's
short, but long enough to shine blue-black as the light catches
it—dead-straight parting, a hint of that cologne Italian barbers use,
with the retro label on the bottle. He studies me for a moment,
then nods, as though I've passed some test. 'Good morning,' he
says, his Italian accent strong but clear. Before I can answer he's
out of the door.

'Who was that?' I pretend to swoon.

'My new private,' Teddy says, leaning against his classroom door,
jerking a Winston from the packet. 'He's a journalist. Freelance.'
He pauses. 'Guess what he's got in his briefcase.'

'A scoop?'

A longer pause. 'A gun.'

'He says.'

Teddy grins. 'He showed me.'

We walk down the stairs and out into Piazzale Loreto. Our students keep telling us that Mussolini and his mistress were hung here by their heels. Yes, we say, we know. They don't seem proud of it, or indignant, though some of them were alive when it happened. It's history by now.

'It's got a silencer. And it's loaded.'

'Is that allowed?'

'He showed me a licence,' says Teddy.

Most of the tables outside the bar are taken but there's one in the sun that nobody wants. We sit and order beers.

'Is that all he showed you?' I say, not wanting to sound waspish. 'It doesn't sound as though you're using the Method.'

'He's too interesting for that,' says Teddy, shielding his eyes with his hand. 'He's got to protect himself. It's big business. He can't exactly say what he does. It's pretty dangerous stuff.'

'He tells you this in English?'

Teddy looks sheepish. 'Not all of it, no. We piece it together. His French is good.'

I light the last cigarette from his packet. 'You're sure he isn't trying to impress you? As in pick you up?'

Teddy crushes the packet, drops it into his empty glass. 'Calm down, Simon, he isn't gay. He's married, actually. He's got two kids.'

I close my eyes for a moment, feeling the start of a headache. But I won't be shaken off.

'How old is he?'

'Twenty-seven.' Teddy doesn't say it but I know we both think the same thing. Four years older than we are. Four years between us and a real life—a wife, two kids. A licensed gun in the briefcase.

'What's his name?'

'Luigi.'

'Luigi what?'

Teddy squints for a moment, as if considering whether to tell me.

'Baietto.'

Three days later I'm given a new class. A mother and two children. I realise who they are when I see the family together in the corridor. She's my height, slightly taller than her husband, dark as he is, with hair pinned up loosely, tendrilling down her neck, and suntanned arms and shoulders. The children, both boys, are oddly blond, like Finns. One of them looks seven or eight, the other maybe three years younger. Baietto shakes my hand, then introduces me. His wife's Anna; the boys are Davide and Luca. He knows my name. I smile and nod, sweating in the close air of the school. 'Look after them for me, Simon,' he says, smiling. His canines are longer than the other teeth, set higher in the gums.

In the classroom, Anna sits in the middle, with Davide on one side and Luca, the younger boy, on the other. I stand behind my desk as I've been told, the timer set for fifty minutes, the Method open in front of me. I've never taught children before. Anna's wearing a simple white dress, her knees just visible as she smoothes the fabric round her, brown and slightly gleaming. When she smiles, a keen smile filled with trust, her lips part and I have to look away; she seems so open, so available. She sits between her sons and waits for me to teach them.

They are the most beautiful family I have ever seen. I'm awestruck as I point at the table and say table, point at the chair and say chair. Table, they say, and chair. If I knew what else to do, I'd close the Method and teach them what they need, whatever that might be.

The boys' feet don't even touch the floor.

I pester Teddy to tell me about Baietto. He's something high up in business, the world we glimpse when we teach the Method to middle management in offices with plasterboard walls and Venetian-blinded windows. He spends weekends in the villas of the rich and powerful. It's a world of private jets and sleaze, and not quite his. Not yet. He's cagey about what he does, or Teddy is.

In return, Teddy wants to hear about Baietto's wife. She's an absolute beginner, I say, but quick to learn. I do this to tease him, because what he really needs is the kind of detail I'd like supplied by him about her husband, but don't dare ask for. The texture of his skin, the way he smells. Teddy, in any case, wouldn't have a clue how to answer, unlike me. I tell him she likes to play with the shoulder straps of her dress, and how she pouts when she's working out the answer. Mostly, the boys are well behaved despite the tedium of the Method, but when they aren't she sinks onto her haunches in front of them and flirts until they're good. He closes his eyes, imagining the scene. 'We should swap,' I say, hopefully, but Teddy wants all of them, the adults at least. 'You could keep the kids,' he says, magnanimous.

'They've got a place on Lake Garda,' he announces one evening, over our usual dinner—plates of spaghetti with oil and garlic, a one-and-a-half litre plastic bottle of draught Barbera. We're sitting in the kitchen of our cold-water flat. Our room's next door, a single bed in one corner, a sofa in the other. 'It overlooks the lake,' he continues. We weren't talking about the Baietto family but I know immediately who he means.

'I get the impression she's rich,' I say. 'I think the money's hers.'

Teddy shrugs. 'He's got a sports car, a little two-seater red job. She must have bought it for him.' It's hard not to hear the envy in his voice.

'Maybe they'll ask us to go with them one weekend,' I say, to cheer him up.

'He's got a boat as well,' says Teddy.

I wake up during the night to find myself scratching a mosquito bite on my hand. We've rigged up a curtain across the window, to keep out insects, but it slides off the broom handle during the night and gathers on the floor. I lie on my side and try not to think of the dawn light flooding in and the itch on the back of my finger. I'm sleeping on the sofa because I'm two inches shorter than Teddy and just fit the space between the arms if I bend my legs. The sheet I'm lying on sticks to me as I move. I glance across at Teddy, breathing heavily in the opposite corner of the room, and see that his upper sheet has slipped off him entirely. He's on his back, stark naked, his arms moving up and down as though, in his dream, he's coaxing something towards him, or climbing. I walk across the warm tiles until I'm by his bed. He's muttering in an anxious way, but I can't make out the words, and don't want to. I'm scared he might be talking to some dream me. Not thinking what I'm doing, I pick up his sheet from the floor. I'm about to cover him with it when he opens his eyes to stare at me, as though he's never been asleep.

Anna arrives five minutes early, the boys behind her in matching sailor suits. I'm standing in the corridor and she comes across to me in a way that makes me think she wants a cigarette. I haven't seen her smoke, but almost every Milanese does. I'm about to hold out my packet of Winston when she halts my arm with her hand and asks me, in her careful English, if we'd like to come to Lake Garda for the weekend. Except that I don't know if she means we or me, because that's the awful thing about English. Me? I say, my finger on my chest. No, you, she says, laughing, shaking her hair and looking around as if for Teddy. *Voi*, she says, just to make sure I've understood, and I laugh. Yes, I say. Thank you. Yes. We'd love to.

It turns out that her husband has asked Teddy independently, as though we've been shared out between them. We check they mean the same weekend; they do. A regatta of some sort will be taking place, and Teddy will be helping Baietto with his boat. What about me? I wonder.

We arrange to meet in Piazzale Loreto, outside the school. It's just after half past five in the morning. Teddy and I have had coffee and brioches in a bar at the station. I'm buzzing, as though I haven't slept at all. Arriving in the square, we spot Baietto—call him Luigi, hisses Teddy—with his elbow on the roof of a red MG Spider; he's short enough to do this without seeming ridiculous. He's not wearing a suit, but his casual clothes, a crisply ironed seersucker shirt and knee-length khaki shorts, have the same formality. His legs are wiry, dark with sun and hair. He's wearing boat shoes and no socks, as we are. We walk across. He stands up straight, his hard brown hand extended.

'Anna arrives very soon,' he says, establishing that we'll be speaking English. It's the barter economy of leisure time with students: language for food. 'Women,' he sighs, then grins his wolfish grin. He squeezes Teddy's arm. 'You are with me,' he says to him, which means I'm not. 'We shall discuss tactics of the regatta in the journey.'

A few minutes later, a steel-grey Alfa Romeo pulls up beside us. Anna winds down her window and smiles at Luigi, and then at me. She reaches across to open the passenger door and I get in beside her. Lifting a finger to her lips, she nods towards the boys, asleep in the back, Luca curled against Davide, one arm across his stomach. They're dressed like their father, button-down shirts and tailored shorts, bare sun-tanned legs. Anna's wearing a pale green miniskirt and a low-cut lemon blouse I've seen in a window in Via Montenapoleone. I notice these things in a way I never did before Milan. I've become a reader of labels in coats. I spot Pollini shoes from twenty yards and can tell you how much they cost.

Anna drives fast and well, as we pass through the sleeping suburbs towards the motorway. We play tag with the Spider for a while, overtaking, being overtaken back, Teddy's exhilarated face grinning out as the smaller car sweeps ahead. But as soon as we pass the toll booth and head east towards the lake, we're left behind. Anna lights herself a cigarette from a packet on the dash, offering me one five seconds later with a murmur of apology. Both of us try to talk at first, but it's too much like hard work. She seems to be happy to concentrate on her driving, answering my occasional questions with a nod or a shake of her head. She's pulled her hair back into a pony tail, which makes her look younger than usual. She could be my age, I think, if it weren't for the children.

We've been travelling for twenty minutes when Luca wakes up and says he wants to *fare la pipi*. 'I'm sorry,' she says. 'We stop for coffee and *pipi*?' Two kilometres on, she pulls into an Autogrill with professional assurance.

'You wait there,' she tells me, pointing at the entrance to the bar, 'with Davide.' She takes Luca by the hand and half-carries half-drags him, grumpy with tiredness, towards the toilets. Davide, wide awake, leads the way to the bar, his manner a parody of his father's as he holds the door open, unnervingly well-mannered. We walk past the local delicacies, miniature hams, wedges of cheese, salamis dangling on strings. Davide looks with longing at a tube of Baci, and then at me. 'Do you like chocolates?' I ask him. He nods.

I'm about to pay when Anna arrives and takes the tube from my hand. 'This is for Davide, yes?' she says, Luca dangling tetchily from her waist.

'Yes, but I want to buy them,' I say. 'As a present.'

'No.' She seems genuinely annoyed. I watch her take out a large green leather wallet. She pays for the tube of Baci and coffees for us both, then puts the Baci in her bag. We drink in silence. As soon as we've finished she gives me her most brilliant smile. '*Andiamo*,' she says.

I expected a villa overlooking the lake, Liberty or older, Palladian even, a lawn rolling down to the water's edge, a boathouse maybe. But we park outside a stuccoed four-storey residential block that must have been built in the 1960s, halfway down a long street filled with similar buildings. Anna tells the boys to carry in the bags from the boot. I hover with my almost empty rucksack, waiting to be told what to do. 'Come,' she says. I follow her into the foyer.

The flat is on the third floor. Two bedrooms, one for the parents, the other, with bunk beds, for the boys. The bathroom's cramped, an electric water heater cantilevered over the tub. After sleeping in the same room as Teddy for six months, I'd imagined guest rooms, one each, and endless hot water.

Teddy and Luigi are standing on a balcony facing the lake, a sliver of blue between the buildings opposite. As they greet us, Luigi squeezes Teddy's shoulder and I know that Teddy doesn't notice this, or that, if he does, he attaches no importance to what is, after all, no more than a simple gesture of companionship—the way men are between themselves. It's a language I can't speak without the words changing sense. I reveal myself somehow; I get the accent wrong.

'We're sleeping in here,' Teddy says, and points to a sofa like the one I sleep on in Milan.

'It opens,' says Luigi, quickly. 'It's matrimonial.'

'Double,' says Teddy. 'We say double.'

Anna slices bread and spreads Nutella thickly onto the slices. Standing, we drink milky coffee, which I hate, and eat the over-sweet concoction. Teddy and I listen to a conversation we understand in patches; family business, homework that has to be done, a woman who didn't bring Luigi's suits back from the cleaners. It's still only breakfast time; the whole day stretches ahead. I wish I'd stayed in Milan.

Ten minutes later, Teddy and Luigi leave.

I find myself part of a group of boating widows and their children. We're in Riva del Garda. It's the best place on the lake for wind, I'm told by Marilena, one of the women, and I see the small expensive boats whipping across the white-flecked water in what looks like utter chaos. Luca, excited, points and shouts, *papà*, but Davide slaps him gently round the back of the head, so presumably he's mistaken. We're standing on the battlements of a fortress that once belonged to the Scaligeri, Marilena tells me, then waits for me to ask who they were. She doesn't appear to have any children; she's latched onto me physically, her fingers—tanned into a wrinkled pelt—gripping my forearm. Anna is staring out over the water, her elbows on the wall.

'*Bello*,' she says in a dreamy voice, and I agree. '*Bello*.' But that's as far as it goes. I turn back to Marilena. 'The Scaligeri?' I say.

'The rulers of Verona. Do you know Verona?'

'No, I don't.'

'*Non conosce Verona*,' she announces, appalled, to the other women, who, as one, inform me:

'*Verona è bella, molto bella*.'

'*Tutto è bello in Italia*,' I say, but my sarcasm's lost. Well, of course it is. It isn't seen as sarcasm. What I've said is the simple truth.

After lunch, Anna takes us to Sirmione, where we climb to the top of a similar castle and stare across another section of the lake. The small boats continue to dart and scud, but at a distance. Davide is in a filthy mood; he must be as bored as I am. Luca is whining and hangs from his mother's arm as if he's losing the use of his legs. Anna has given up trying to make conversation, but appears to be perfectly content. I caught her watching me over lunch, as I ate my spaghetti, and her cheeks flushed slightly beneath the tan as she stood up to collect the boys' plates. She's an extraordinary colour, glowing and even, too cosmetic to be true. I look at her slim brown hands now, resting on the stone wall as we lean over and stare at a faraway boat that may contain her husband and my best, my only friend, and think that one day she'll have the leathery claws of Marilena. Davide will have a paunch and Luca will be bald. And then we'll all be dead.

The regatta hasn't gone as well as Luigi hoped. We have dinner together round the same small table we used for breakfast. Anna has ordered pizzas, but six boxes take up too much room and Davide and Luca are sent to the sofa with theirs, where they fight until their father snaps at them to stop. Luigi is noisy, ebullient, aggrieved. He makes no effort to speak English, complaining to Anna in more or less comprehensible Italian about the currents, the weather, the state of the boat, the other competitors. Teddy, in a jocular, back-slapping way, as though he's supposed to welcome it, also comes in for criticism. At one point, Luigi refers to him, with a mock-solemn face that only confirms his irritation, as *il mio povero inglesino.* My poor little Englishman. All the same, the man has a vigour coming off him I can't not find attractive. Even the way he tears at the pizza with his sharp white teeth is sexy. Before we sat down to eat, he'd showered and wandered naked round the living room, his body heavier, less hairy, than I'd imagined, his cock not quite soft, plump and bouncing as he dried his ears with a towel and whistled for Anna to bring him underwear: Y-fronts and a vest, both pristine white, both ironed. Basically, he's a shit, I think now, as he stretches his arms in the air and imitates someone climbing rigging, then shakes his hands around, to loosen up. 'Time for bed,' he announces. And so, of course, it is.

Teddy and I lie on the wafer-thin mattress, almost touching, despite our efforts not to, mine as much as his. There's absolute silence for maybe fifteen, twenty minutes and then the sound through the wall of Anna and Luigi making love, muffled giggling, squeaking springs, a barely suppressed groan that must be Luigi's, a bang of the bed-head against the plaster. It could be funny, but isn't; I don't know what Teddy's thinking, but what I feel is a muddle of melancholy and loneliness, as though I'll never be understood. When Anna creeps into the bathroom to piss, we pretend to be asleep. It seems to go on for hours.

'I wish we hadn't come,' whispers Teddy as soon as she's back in their bedroom. 'I've had a fucking awful day.'

'Me too,' I say. 'Good night.'

'Good night.'

It must be almost dawn when I'm woken by something and open my eyes. Luigi is standing beside our sofa bed, naked, looking down at us both. When he sees me stare at him, he makes a pistol with his right hand and fires at me, then grins, and returns to his room.

Luigi and Teddy go off after an early breakfast, Luigi freshly showered and bristling with energy, Teddy glancing wretchedly towards me as they leave, as though I should block their way. Anna takes the dirty plates from me with a tut-tut when I try to help clear the table, so I sit between the boys and pick up one of their *Topolino* comic books from the floor, thumbing through it, translating the occasional speech bubble. Luca, to my astonishment, springs onto my lap and asks me to read it out loud. Amused, I do as I'm told, and only stop when Anna tells him to leave me alone.

'It's okay,' I say, 'I like it. But she ignores me, as Luca does her. She rushes across to the sofa and tugs at Luca, who throws his arms round my neck. Before I know what's happening, Anna has lost her footing and the three of us are sprawled in a heap, with Luca between us and Anna's hair in my face. Struggling back to her feet, her elbow digs into my groin and I double over, gasping with pain, as Luca wriggles off.

'*Mio Dio,*' she says, over and over again, clutching her face. '*Mi dispiace.*'

As soon as I get my breath back, I shake my head. 'Okay,' I say, my voice sounding strange to me. 'I'm fine.'

She cries to the boys, asking them how to say sorry in English, how do you say it, she can't remember, she's an idiot.

Two hours later, we're on the western bank of the lake, in Salò. The only sign of the small town's bump with history are the racks of postcards with Mussolini's grim square face staring skywards, and one or two shops with miniature mass-produced busts of Il Duce next to Michelangelo's *David* and the Colosseum. At the lakeside, Anna takes me to a bar and we sit while the boys choose ice cream. The waiter comes to our table and asks me what we want, but Anna orders aperitivi before I have a chance to answer. As soon as he's gone, she looks at me.

'Are you happy?' she asks.

'Happy?' I'm not sure what she means. Now? At this minute? With my life?

'With him,' she says.

'With Teddy?'

She nods. I'm still not sure what to say, where to start or not to start. I wonder what she thinks. That we're lovers? Is that what she'd like to hear? That I think he's bored and would like to go home? That I'm bored too? Finally, I say, 'Yes.'

'*È naturale. È dolce*,' she says and then, maybe to show she can, translates herself. 'He is sweet.'

'And are you happy?' I say, less out of curiosity–though curiosity's part of it–than from a desire to direct the conversation elsewhere. 'With Luigi?'

The waiter arrives with our drinks, a small bowl of olives, some crisps. He doesn't go at once: perhaps he wants to be paid and doesn't know who to ask. But Anna ignores him until he leaves, then sighs. 'Luigi is a good man,' she says, taking an olive. 'A good father.'

'Yes.' I'd ask her if he's also a good husband, but I hear the sound of their fucking last night, his climactic moan. It isn't all there is, and it isn't what my question would have meant. Still, fucking must count for something. 'That's very important,' I say.

I have the feeling she'll tell me more, but Luca and Davide run to the table and come to a sudden halt, their arms raised in a fascist salute, giggling. Anna leaps to her feet and slaps them both, hard. Luca bursts into tears. Davide's face turns purple. I sip my fluorescent orange aperitivo and eat some crisps.

The regatta went better today. There's a shared-joke sort of camaraderie between Luigi and Teddy that we're all witness to as Anna serves up pasta round the crowded table. Luigi fills and refills our glasses with Bardolino, from the shores of the lake, he tells us more than once, kissing the bunched tips of his fingers in faked ecstasy. *Mamma mia*, he says. He's in his vest and his bare arm brushes against mine a dozen times and I can't not think about the rest of his body, which means I'm eating with a hard-on. I wonder idly if he'd fuck Teddy, now they're such great boating buddies—assuming Teddy was up for it, which, of course, he isn't. Or isn't with me. I wonder, less idly, if Luigi would fuck me. He would if I were Anna, I think, stupidly, drunk. She's sweating as she stirs the pasta round the last few drops of sauce in the bowl before raising it into the air and looking around the table, at me, *at me*, to see who wants it. Anna would fuck me, I think. She's hot and tired, her armpits damp, her hair in a tangle, fractious after that business with the boys and who knows what else, what other slights she might have received that I don't notice. Anna would fuck me.

We're driving back to Milan after we've eaten; not, as planned, tomorrow. Luigi has important business early in the morning, he tells us, slipping on his shirt, adjusting a holster for a gun I wasn't sure he'd brought. Was he armed on the boat? I wonder. Is he always armed? What does it mean to be always armed? To be strong? Anna makes coffee for the adults and packs some cartons of juice and biscuits into a bag for Davide and Luca. We walk down to the street together, and I still don't know who paid for these lavish, status-ridden cars or the poky, ill-equipped flat that seems to belong to no one. It's one of the mysteries of the weekend I'll talk about later with Teddy, who is bending himself, stiffly, into the passenger seat of Luigi's Spider. For the second time today, he glances across at me and this time the look on his face is almost comically one of panic. I wave, a silly wave, not sure what else to do. 'See you in Milan,'

I shout as the car pulls away from the kerb and disappears, at speed, round the corner. It's almost dark. For a second, with the image of Luigi's gun, of Luigi's smile, still in my head, I think, we'll all be killed.

'*Milano*,' Anna corrects me. Her little joke.

By the time we're on the motorway, the light has gone from the sky and the boys are fast asleep in the back of the car, Davide slumped against the door, Luca's head in his lap. Luca's already in his pyjamas, so he won't need to be woken. Once more, we try to talk, but after a mile or so Anna turns on the radio. '*Ti piace la musica?*' she asks, as an afterthought, and I say, 'Yes, I like music'.

The station she tunes into is playing jazz: Keith Jarrett, Chick Corea. It's not what I'd choose, but it feels right as she drives, her hands relaxed on the wheel, her shoes kicked off, as fast as the limit will allow and then a little faster, keeping up with the flow of the other cars, overtaking, being overtaken, a shuffle of engines and rubber and steel that is oddly silent, oddly genteel, the merest pantomime of power. I relax. Nothing bad can happen to us, I think.

When Davide's breathing changes I turn to see how he is and Anna notices, and smiles. 'You would be a good father,' she says. Before I can answer—or find an answer—she starts to sing to the track on the radio and I realise that the words she is singing are English, though I'm not sure what they mean. The song's by Joni Mitchell, it's called *All I Want*, but I don't know who's playing this version. After a moment, I start to sing along with Anna. She's startled: perhaps she didn't know what she was doing, perhaps she's forgotten I'm here beside her. I know the whole song, I discover, as though I've learnt it on purpose, for this moment, on this lonely road, incomplete, the best in me and in everyone still waiting to be discovered.

After a while, she stops to listen and I sing on to the end, my voice low so as not to wake the children, word perfect. Until the music ends.

'*Bello,*' she says. '*Che bello.*'

Danny Rhodes is the other of two novels, Asboville *and* Soldier Boy. *Both books received critical acclaim, and I'm delighted to be able to include one of his stories here.*

A Covering of Leaves

Danny Rhodes

Each morning brought a fresh covering of leaves. Webster had the job of clearing them, first from the platform, then from the entrance lobby, and given time, from the station's guttering and drains. In between these tasks, he was meant to oversee the car park. He did not have to clear the leaves from the line, nor did he have to explain to irate passengers why leaves could cause a train to be delayed, but he did the second job anyhow.

'It's mainly to do with the points,' he'd say. 'They get clogged up with fallen leaves. There's nothing we can do about it except clear them when they begin to cause obstruction, for safety reasons of course.'

Things had changed in the past few days. There had been a crash at the city station. The crash had killed forty-seven people. It might have killed a whole lot more, but it had only maimed and injured the rest, some two hundred all told.

Webster could see the front page of a tabloid in the kiosk across from him. It showed a station clock, its bent hands and charred face crudely displaying the time the engine had exploded into a ball of flame, twenty-three minutes past eight, right slap bang in the middle of commuter hour. In the background of the picture, the paint had been stripped from the walls by the blast. The blistered paint that remained was clinging to the walls precariously, like so many autumn leaves.

For Webster it meant a quiet week. He found himself with too much time on his hands. He liked to keep busy, to stop his mind from wandering. When it wandered it tended to wander back to the time before his own world had fallen apart.

The day after the crash he had come to work as normal, only to wind up twiddling his thumbs as a small and silent trickle of passengers entered the station. He found himself searching the faces of these people, looking for signs. One man arrived with his briefcase in his hand and his long cashmere coat draped over his forearm as always. He flashed his travel card as always. On his face was a white piece of cotton wool, held in place by a surgical plaster. He might have cut himself shaving or he might have survived a train crash by the skin of his teeth. In his mind, Webster played back the moment where a tiny shard of metal from the train cut into the man's cheek. The briefcase looked scarred and scratched too, like it had been battered and bruised over many years, or flung across a platform full of broken glass. It was funny how it all worked, how one man could escape with a cut cheek and another man lose a leg or an arm. It was funny how some lived and some died. But then Webster knew all about that. He knew more about that than most.

There were others: a woman who might have been limping, a man who could have been holding his arm in a peculiar position. These were the hard core, defiantly stepping up into their working lives the very next day, stoically treating the event as nothing more than a minor disruption, just more leaves on the line. Others came in the days that followed. And when the station announcement was made that the train would be delayed due to leaves on the line, nobody flinched. They simply stood on the platform and waited, as always.

But for Webster, things were changing.

It started when he noticed the cars. Two were nestled together under an ancient oak in the middle of the car park: a brand new black BMW and a silver Honda Civic. A third was by the iron fencing that separated the platform from the car park. It was a metallic blue Range Rover and it had a faded sticker in the back window that read 'Burgreen Horse Trials 2004'. The final car was a small red Nissan, parked way off on its own in the bottom corner. It was parked in the sort of space that would only be used by the last person to arrive on any given morning, or by somebody who wanted to be out of the way of everybody else. It was the Nissan that Webster felt drawn to the most. When he arrived at the Nissan on the morning after the crash, when he saw the golden leaves on the bonnet, the day old ticket in the window, the stubbed out cigarette in the open ashtray, it dawned on him that he might be staring at the possessions of a dead person.

On the second day, Webster spent several minutes examining the cars. He built pictures of lives. It was the sort of game a man played when his job required no thought at all and when thinking brought up moments best left alone. His mind leaned mostly towards the Nissan cowering sadly in the corner. More leaves had fallen, turning the paintwork a shade darker, creating some kind of curious camouflage.

The Range Rover wasn't there when Webster arrived on the third day, and the BMW was collected by a pickup at lunch while

Webster was eating his sandwiches. The Honda went in the afternoon. Webster watched from the office window as a middle-aged man approached the car park, skirted it slowly, and finally stopped at the Civic's window. Part of him wanted to rush up to the man and enquire about the Civic's owner, but the casualty list scared him. This was not the owner of the car. This was a man collecting a car for somebody else. This might be a man collecting his daughter's car for instance. She might be a casualty. She might be a fatality.

When the Civic had gone, Webster watched the rain fall. It came down hard and heavy, plastering fallen leaves to the Nissan in the corner by the black railings. The rainwater ran off the roof and down the windscreen in a torrent, ran along the edge of the bonnet and then dripped from the wheel arches like tears. Webster felt himself crying too.

On the Thursday morning a thin rain fell, a delicate veil. Webster was skulking around the car park, thinking about the news he'd listened to on the radio, the facts and figures, when he arrived once more at the Nissan. Its roof was covered in soggy leaves now, as was the bonnet. But the windscreen was clear. The leaves were bunched up at the edges, and there were two clear arcs across the glass. A single leaf fell and rested upon the windscreen. Webster stared at it. The orphan leaf brought the others into focus. The wipers had been running. There was no other explanation. And Webster noticed something else too. The bonnet was steaming, the way bonnets sometimes steam in the rain when the heat of the engine has warmed the metal. Webster reached out and pressed his palm on the bonnet. It was warm to the touch.

It was later that morning when it truly started. The sun had come out. The leaves had begun to dry. Webster heard an engine cough into life. It was an older engine. It was coming from the far end of the car park. Three times the engine spluttered and died, but the fourth time it held and started to tick over. Webster turned. He was thinking of heartbeats. Sure enough, the Nissan was reversing out of the space. It swung back, stopped, the gears crunched and then it started up between the avenues of cars towards him. Webster watched it cruise past him, stared at it and felt his world turn upside down; not because there was no driver—he already knew that would be the case—but because he felt an urgent connection. Way back, in the time before, he had connected to Alice in much the same way, easily, naturally, with no effort at all. Now it was happening again.

Webster ran across the car park to his own car.

He followed the Nissan through the town, the bright, crisp sunlight reflecting off the red paintwork and the chrome bumper in such a way that the car now looked pristine and polished, as though it had not been parked in a station car park for days at all, as though it had just rolled off the production line that very morning. It was ridiculous, because the Nissan was at least ten years old, perhaps fifteen, but as Webster followed it the feeling grew inside of him that something special was happening. He could sense a change in everything. The town seemed different. It felt, and this was so ridiculous that Webster hardly let the notion stick before subduing it, that he was driving through the town as it used to be, as it was in the time before...

The Nissan was still ahead, gleaming brilliantly in the light. There were people on the streets, people chatting, mothers with children, young men and women, the elderly, all going about their daily business. The statue on the green was still there, standing ceremony over everything. It was just as Webster had always known it to be.

He'd grown up in this town. He knew the place. He had memories of the green, amongst the flowers, under the canopy of the trees. He remembered the summers mostly, lounging there under the shadow of the old clock on the town hall, watching the girls. He remembered sitting under those same trees with Alice, her with her head on his chest, in the summers before.

He remembered when the local council announced their plans to have the trees removed. It was necessary, they'd said. The trees were crowding each other. There was the problem of cleaning up leaves in Autumn. Some trees had to be removed in order for others to flourish.

Except it was ten years ago when the change had been made, and today Webster was staring vacantly at the old green, staring at the dark shadows on the lawn where the trees arced, the blanket of leaves, two children kicking up the leaves, which fell back to earth in that graceful, multicoloured way, sending red, yellow and golden light in all directions.

The Nissan was at a red light, in the filter lane, indicating to turn right, to head up and out of town along the artery that ran to the hills. Webster's heart skipped a beat. The filter lane had been phased out ten years ago, to make way for a roundabout. Webster negotiated it every morning on the way to work. But here was the filter lane, as clear as day. Here were the lights, changing now, through the amber colour of autumn leaves to green. The roundabout was still just a planning proposal on a scrap of paper in the council offices. It hadn't happened yet. So many things hadn't happened yet.

The Nissan pressed forwards in the traffic. It was a new model. Webster could see that now, bright and shining and new, inching forward amongst the cars, looking proud, passing people at the traffic island, nobody batting an eyelid, nobody seeing what he could see, that the car was empty, that there was nobody driving it. Was he going mad? Had it all finally got the better of him? Latent stress they called it, when the physical effects come about so long after the time when the stressful event took place.

He was on Scotland Road now. The houses grew in size and stature here, in tandem with the gentle gradient of the hill. The property value increased too. Nothing had changed up here in a long time. It might have been ten years earlier or it might have been the present. The Nissan looked older again, but that might have been the shadows that were cast by the line of trees on each side of the road. The gutters were full of leaves. They were thick and soggy, just a black pulpy mass. The freshly fallen leaves, the crisper leaves, were sent dancing into the air by the Nissan as it disturbed them. The parked cars at the side of the road were hidden, each one disguising its true age, under a covering of leaves.

Webster looked down at the petrol gauge. The little arrow was already pointing to red. He would not be able to stop and get petrol without losing the Nissan. These anxieties were pressing on his mind when the Nissan swung out into the road and turned into a driveway. Webster pulled up at the kerbside. He turned off the engine and waited. This was a little awkward. He couldn't follow the car up the drive. He suddenly had notions of there being a driver after all. The empty seat, the trees on the green, the filter lane, these things were already distant. Could he be certain he'd seen them? Wasn't it possible that he was hallucinating, remembering how things had once been? Wishing? Hoping? Remembering the time before?

Webster climbed out of the car and walked to the end of the driveway. The driveway was covered in leaves. They were falling even as he stared ahead of himself, in ones and twos, in groups, falling to the ground, spinning and twirling in the sunshine, in the shadows, resting on top of other leaves, forming a carpet. Through the leaves was a set of tracks, two lanes of crushed leaves where the Nissan had been just a minute earlier. The driveway turned gently to the right, disappearing into the trees. Feeling nauseous, a growing uncertainty in his stomach, Webster chose to follow it down.

The house was smaller than he'd expected. It was nestled amongst the trees, the branches curving around and over it like some protective mechanism. Webster got the impression that the house was trying to hide from him, but the sparsely leafed autumn branches were not up to the task like they might have been in high summer. Still, in their own way the leaves were trying. The roof was covered in them, the guttering holding them in piles against the slope, giving the house soft lines where hard edges would usually be. Between the porch and the half-moon gravelled area where the Nissan was now parked, the leaves had formed a wall where they'd been blown up against the steps. It was a good foot high. To reach the door somebody would have to kick them out of the way, leave some sort of trail, but the leaves had not been disturbed at all. Webster looked at the Nissan. It was empty. He walked across the carpet of leaves and pressed his head to the driver's window. There was nobody hiding inside. He felt ridiculous for even thinking as much.

Webster skirted around the house, his feet trampling fallen leaves.

The kitchen was new. The cooker was built into the units and the sink still retained its shine. There was evidence of life. On the worktop was a plate carrying a half-eaten piece of toast, beside the plate a mug of tea, half drunk. Webster could see the white ring in the tea where the milk had separated. How many days had it been there? Two? Three? Webster caught a vision of himself in the kettle, an elongated reflection, alien in shape and an alien here in this garden. It caused him to stop for a moment. What was he doing? Part of him, the part that was responsible for his own self-preservation, was nagging at him to get away from the place, but a larger part of him was eager to extend the moment. Something was calling him. He had to answer.

He lifted his gaze to look past the kitchen and down the hallway. Through the frosted glass of the front door, Webster could see the bright red hue of the Nissan. On the floor under the letterbox were several unopened items of mail. That was the observation that tilted him back into reality.

When he reached the front of the house, he noticed a change. The passenger door to the Nissan was open, beckoning him. There was something warm about the interior of the Nissan, something comforting. He'd felt it the first time he'd seen it. Now he found himself walking towards the open door, his feet ploughing through the densely piled leaves. Already he could see two leaves on the passenger seat. Others were falling onto the car roof, onto the bonnet, giving the car an unkempt look. And it was true that the Nissan looked less new once again, looked as though it had seen some things, been to places, lived, much as he had seen some things, been to places, much as he had lived, especially recently. My God, he had learned about living recently, learned about the hard act of living, grinding out each day with a heavy weight holding him down and a darkness threatening, darkness around every corner, darkness waiting for him at home, darkness everywhere. He looked up at the windows of the house. There was the same darkness here, the same empty darkness. It was unmistakeable.

And yet there was light too.

Webster rested his hands on the door frame. A sensation ran through him, one of familiarity and togetherness.

'If this were a person...then perhaps...'

Perhaps there wouldn't be another autumn like that one. Perhaps there wouldn't be a smothering of leaves. Perhaps the road would not be so wet. Perhaps he would insist on driving Alice to work. Perhaps...

Webster settled into the passenger seat. It felt good, fitted his contours like a favourite old armchair. He felt the sun on his face, a warming sensation that ran through to the very heart of his being. More leaves were falling, brown, yellow, golden in colour, the light playing off them in a million ways, a stained glass window effect. Here he was in this cathedral. He felt the darkness rising from within him, choked out by the kaleidoscopic light. He understood now. The car was reaching out to him, reaching out for somebody to lean on, somebody who knew what it meant to lose all that you have in the world in the blink of an eye. He reached across for the steering wheel and caressed it gently. His fingers felt at home there. When the Nissan purred into life at its own accord, Webster didn't jump in amazement. He simply closed his eyes and relaxed. He let his mind drift to a vision of Alice on their wedding day. He pictured her smile, a perfect smile in a perfect moment.

Webster opened his eyes on a congregation of leaves. He pulled the passenger door shut, but didn't bother fastening the seatbelt. The Nissan reversed over fallen leaves and gently made its way down the driveway. There was a journey ahead for both of them, Webster knew that much, a journey that would end on a road covered in wet autumn leaves. There might, for a brief moment, be some pain, but after that anything was surely possible.

Ben Cheetham's story is one of the longer pieces in this volume, but you get the sense that it could easily have been longer still: Finn could spend hundreds of pages wandering through a sort of Dickensian episodic series of characters and conflicts. Perhaps it's just as well Ben kept it short, though, or we'd never have managed to fit it in here.

Sometimes the Only Way Out is In

Ben Cheetham

The wind shrieked like a monster against Finn's bedroom window. That was one of the worst things about living in a high-rise. The noise of wind was always there. It lessened to a whisper sometimes, but it always returned to batter at the grimy, weather-stained panes. Sometimes, lying in bed at night, Finn heard angry voices in it. 'It's your fault,' they shouted. 'It's your fault he left.' If he felt really brave, which wasn't very often, Finn shouted back, 'Go away, wind, and leave me alone.' Most of the time, he pulled the covers over his head and sought reassurance from Zack, the boy who lived in his mouth. *Take no notice of the wind*, Zack would say. *The wind is a big fat liar.*

The best thing about living in a high-rise was the view. Finn could sit staring at the view for hours of an evening. From his bedroom window, which looked towards the setting sun, he could see other high-rises poking up like rows of dirty, uneven teeth. He could see rigid lines of maisonette blocks and terraced houses, and sinuous lines of detached houses with big gardens. He could see traffic-clogged roads, crisscrossing in every direction. Further out, he could see more high-rises, more houses, more roads. And further out still, he could see yet more of the same, stretching away, on and on, seemingly to infinity.

Finn knew the city didn't go on forever, though. He knew that somewhere out there was a place where all around you, all you could see were fields, trees and hills. And he knew that that place was called Wales. His mum and dad had taken him there once, four years earlier. They'd spent a week camped in a field between a rock-capped hill and the sea. Pretty much all he remembered of that week now was that the sun had shone and the sky had been blue every day, and he'd eaten ice cream on the beach and paddled in the sea, and his parents hadn't argued, not once. But even those memories—the most cherished he possessed—were fading, getting dimmer and dimmer. He might've started to wonder if the holiday was just a happy dream, if it hadn't been for the photo.

Finn assumed his mum had taken the photo, since she wasn't in it. It was of him and his dad sat on deckchairs outside a tent, the steep hillside of heather and rock in the background. Both of them were smiling. He'd spent hour after hour studying it, fixing the smallest details of the scene in his mind. It was the only photo he had left of his dad. His mum had destroyed the rest. He'd salvaged it from the bin and kept it hidden ever since, in a secret place in his bedroom. He usually only took it out late at night, after his mum was in bed. But he knew he was safe to take it out whenever he felt like at the moment. Even though he was late getting up for school, there was no chance his mum would come into his bedroom and find him looking at it, not the state she was in.

You'd better get your clothes on and eat some breakfast, said Zack.

'Aw, why do you always have to be so sensible?' whined Finn.

One of us has to be.

Finn slid the photo back into its hiding place, dressed and made his way to the kitchen. There was nothing much to eat—a few slices of stale bread, but no butter; some scraps of cereal, but no milk. Finn ate the cereal dry with his fingers in front of the telly.

Turn that thing off and brush your teeth, said Zack.

'Awww,' Finn whined again, but he did as Zack said. School rucksack slung over his shoulder, he stood outside his mum's bedroom, listening. There was absolute silence. Very gently, he opened the door. The room was unlit except for a sliver of sunlight that pierced the curtains, and had a heavy, stale atmosphere. A motionless figure was dimly visible on the bed. Finn's mum appeared to be sleeping, but as he padded closer he saw that her eyes were open—open yet unfocused and staring off into some other place.

'Mum,' whispered Finn. No response. 'Mum,' he repeated, louder. Still no response, not even a flicker of an eyelid. He released a sigh that no ten-year old boy should have inside them. She'd been like this for a week now. It had come on suddenly, like last time. Unlike last time, Finn hadn't told anyone else what was happening. He'd tried his best to look after her himself, spoon-feeding her canned chicken soup—he'd heard that was good for you when you were sick—brushing her hair, washing her face with a flannel, even changing her sheets and nightie one time when she wet them.

She's not getting any better, said Zack. *You should tell somebody.*

Finn shook his head fervently. 'They'll put her back in that hospital and make me go live with those people again.'

Those were memories Finn wanted to forget, but which wouldn't go away, no matter how hard he tried to banish them.

Even now, two years later, all he had to do was close his eyes and those memories spooled through his brain like a movie on endless repeat. Memories of his parents arguing for weeks on end, day and night; of his dad slamming out of the flat, shouting that he was never coming back; of his mum sobbing loud enough to make his ears ring; and of her screaming at him, 'My face is fucked up, my skin is fucked up, my figure is fucked up, and it's your fault. It's your fault he's gone.' And finally, memories of her silence and blankness. She'd scared Finn so much that he ran crying next door to Mrs Kelly. Mrs Kelly had phoned a doctor, who contacted Social Services, who placed Finn with a foster family, with whom he lived for half a year until his mum was better. It was the worst time of his life. Every day for the first month he'd expected his dad to turn up and take him home. But he never did. He'd kept asking where his dad was, but nobody seemed to know. It was as if he'd vanished right off the planet.

It was only later on, when he was living back with his mum, that the realisation of where his dad was came to him. He'd been laid in bed, poring over the photo, when a memory of something his dad had said during their holiday suddenly popped into his head. He'd said, 'If I could choose one place to live the rest of my life, this would be it.'

'Can I live here with you, Daddy?' Finn had asked him.

'Of course you can,' he'd replied.

When she got out of hospital, Finn's mum had made him a promise. 'I promise I'll never get sick like that again,' she'd said. And she'd kept that promise, until a week ago. And now, for some reason beyond Finn's understanding, it was happening all over again. Only this time things were going to be different, he was going to make certain of that. He'd made a promise, too, after leaving his foster home, and that promise was that he would never go back into care, not ever, no way, no how, no matter what.

'I'll help you get better, Mum. Don't worry,' Finn said, stroking her arm. 'I've got to go to school now. You stay here and sleep. A nice long sleep will make you feel loads better.'

Remember to get the money for the shopping, said Zack, as Finn turned to leave.

Finn reached into his mum's handbag. There was a tenner and some change in her purse. He pocketed the lot, and after a final worried glance at his mum, left the room. The instant he stepped out the front door, as if she'd been lying in wait for him, Mrs Kelly appeared from her own flat. She was a big old woman with big red lips and an even bigger nose.

'Morning, Finn,' she said, peering over his shoulder into the flat, her eyes homing in like heat-seeking missiles on the pile of dirty bedding left dumped in the hallway. 'Off to school, are you?'

Finn quickly shut the door. 'I'm old enough to walk there by myself now,' he said defensively.

Mrs Kelly looked him up and down, taking in his creased clothes, grubby shirt cuffs and scuffed shoes. 'I can see that.'

Finn didn't like her looking at him like that. It felt as though she was peering right into him. Dropping his gaze away from hers, he stood there shifting his feet uneasily. 'Is your mum around?' she asked.

'She's sleeping.'

'Why is she still sleeping? Is she not feeling well?'

'She's okay. She's just tired.' Finn was quiet a moment, still not looking at Mrs Kelly. Then he said, 'I have to go now or I'll be late. Goodbye, Mrs Kelly.' And he hurried to the stairwell. It was more than two hundred stairs to the ground floor—Finn often tried to count them, but always lost count after two hundred—and the stairwell smelt of wee, but he didn't want to risk Mrs Kelly pursuing him into the lift and asking more questions.

You should tell her, said Zack.

'No I shouldn't,' Finn snapped back. Loudly, as if trying to drown out Zack's voice, he continued, 'No, no, no!'

The shopping—four tins of chicken soup, a sliced white loaf, milk, butter, Lucozade and a Mars bar—sat heavily in Finn's rucksack, making its straps cut into his shoulders as he hurried back to the flat. He jerked to a stop at the front door, his breath catching quickly. The small window at the centre of the door was broken. Shards of glass had been swept into a pile to the side of the door. His first thought was that it must be a burglar—flats were always getting burgled on the estate—but then he heard Mrs Kelly's voice from within. 'It's the boy I feel most sorry for,' she was saying. 'I mean, God, what chance has he got? Sweet bugger all chance, that's what. A few more years of this and he'll end up just like the rest of the kids around here, full of booze and drugs.'

'Well, we're going to do our best to try and make sure that doesn't happen,' replied a woman's voice that Finn also recognised. It belonged to Mrs Sears, the social worker who dealt with his case. The instant he heard it, he guessed pretty much exactly what'd happened. Mrs Kelly, the nosey old cow, had phoned the police, who'd forced entry to the flat and found his mum. And now his mum was back in hospital and Mrs Sears was waiting around to whisk him away to some foster home or other.

Finn felt himself tearing up, both at the thought of his mum in that place that was more like a prison than a hospital and at the thought of being put into care again. Almost savagely, he swiped his tears away. 'No,' he muttered, 'No way am I going back there.'

But where else can you go? asked Zack.

'I can...I...' Finn's face twisted in anxiety. Suddenly an image filled his mind, a shining, sun-drenched image, and he exclaimed in a quiet, excited voice, 'I can go and live with my dad in Wales.'

Don't be silly. You don't even know if your dad really lives in Wales. And even if he does, how will you find him?

'I'll use the photo.'

You haven't got the photo.

'Then I'll get it.'

But–

'Shh,' hissed Finn.

He unhooked the rucksack from his back and, crouching low, crept into the flat. The living-room door was ajar. 'It's a shame,' Mrs Kelly was prattling on now. 'Kiddies should be with their parents. Both their parents, mind you. Kids need a mum and a dad to bring them up properly.'

'Finn will go to a proper home with two parents,' Mrs Sears assured her.

'Yes, but it's not the same, is it?'

'Of course not, but...'

Finn tuned out of the conversation. He couldn't bear to hear anymore. He darted past the door, past his mum's empty bedroom to his room. Carefully so as not to bend it, he retrieved the photo. On his way out, Mrs Sears called from the living room, 'Finn, is that you?'

Finn bolted for the door, snatching up his rucksack on his way to the stairwell. He didn't stop to catch his breath until he was several streets away from the tower block. *What now?* asked Zack.

Finn made no reply. He stared at the photo as if searching for inspiration. 'I know,' he said, suddenly. 'We'll go to the bus station. There must be a bus that goes to Wales.'

Keeping an eye out for Mrs Sears, Mrs Kelly, and any police that might be searching for him, Finn made his way to the bus station. He'd been there plenty of times before with his mum. And like those other times, the station was a milling mass of people, some dashing about, some waiting. He approached the ticket office and asked, 'When's the next bus for Wales?'

'There isn't one, not today anyway,' answered the man behind the glass, tapping at a computer keyboard. 'There's a National Express to Cardiff day after tomorrow, but you can't buy a ticket for that here. You need to go to the National Express office at Victoria Station.'

'But I want to go to Wales today.'

'Then your best bet is to see if there's a train running.' The man eyed Finn curiously. 'Are you here on your own?'

Finn shook his head. 'Thank you,' he said and hurried away.

Back outside, he asked a safe-looking woman for directions to the train station. It took him nearly an hour to walk there, threading his way along crowded pavements that bordered increasingly unfamiliar streets. The air was acrid with the stink of exhaust fumes from cars crawling out of the city centre and grimy, commuter-crammed buses thundering along bus lanes.

The train station was like the bus station, only bigger and busier. Destinations, times and platform numbers flashed up on a huge arrivals and departures board. An echoing voice called out the trains. A stream of bodies carried Finn to the rear of a queue leading to a row of ticket booths. While he waited, he drank the bottle of Lucozade and ate the Mars bar. And he tried not to think about his mum. But he couldn't not think about her. He thought about what it was like visiting her in the hospital: the way you had to wait outside to be buzzed in; the sour disinfectant stink of the corridors; the strange faces and even stranger noises; and, finally, lost somewhere in it all, like a fly caught in a web, his mum. Except the first time he'd visited her, she hadn't seemed much like his mum. She'd been both happier and sadder than his mum. Her eyes had been different again, no longer blank, but not altogether there either. And more than once she'd drifted off into disconnected mutterings, from which Finn was able to pick out bad words like 'bastard' and 'whore'.

Finn felt tears rising to his eyes again. He fought them as hard as he could, but still a few squeezed their way out. 'Can I help you?' asked the ticket seller.

Finn quickly wiped his sleeve over his face. 'I want to go to Wales.'

'Whereabouts in Wales?'

Finn held up the photo. 'There.'

The ticket seller—a tired looking middle-aged man—squinted at the photo. 'Is this a wind up? How am I supposed to know where that is?'

Finn hadn't really expected anyone around here to recognise the place in the photo, but he figured that if he could just get to Wales someone there was bound to. He thought a moment, then asked, 'Is Cardiff near the sea?' When the man nodded, he said, 'I want a ticket to Cardiff, please.'

'One way or return?'

'One way.' Finn didn't intend to return unless his mum got out of hospital, maybe not even then. *Maybe when mum's better she can come live with us in Wales*, he thought.

'One way to Cardiff. That'll be forty-five pounds fifty.'

'Forty-five pounds fifty,' repeated Finn, eyes growing wide. He'd never in his life had that much money at one time. He dug everything he had out of his pockets. 'All I've got is eight quid twenty-two pence.'

'Then you're not going to Cardiff.' Finn looked pleadingly at the ticket seller, but the man was already looking at the next person in line.

His head dropping, Finn trudged away from the ticket booth. *What do we do now?* asked Zack.

Finn shrugged. 'Maybe I could sneak onto the train.'

You'd get caught, and then you'd be in trouble with the police.

Finn heaved a sigh. He stared at the photo, the sunny sky, the grass bending in the sea wind, him and his dad's happy, smiling faces. He wanted to be there more than he'd ever wanted to be anywhere else on earth. 'How far do you reckon it is to Wales?'

Dunno, said Zack. Fifty miles easy.

'Do you think I could walk fifty miles?'

No way could you!

'I think I could.'

Well, you're just stupid then.

'Shut up, Zack.'

I won't shut up. You can't make me either.

'Shut up, shut up, shut up.' Finn's voice rose to a shrill pitch.

A man in a railway uniform materialised out of the crowd. 'Are you okay?' he asked.

Finn flinched and ran out of the station. After several minutes, he looked over his shoulder and saw that he was alone, except for a few dozen other people making their way home or wherever. It gave him a jolt of adrenaline to realise that he was in a completely unfamiliar part of the city. The street was lined with pubs, cafes and restaurants, and busy with people—most of whom were wearing suits—eating and drinking. The sight of them made Finn realise how hungry he was. He opened the loaf and munched on a slice of bread.

Which way was Wales? Zack would know. He always knew stuff like that. 'Zack,' he whispered. No reply. Zack was clearly in a sulk. 'Please, Zack, I'm sorry for shouting.'

A few nervous seconds passed, then to Finn's relief and delight, Zack said, *Remember geography class. Remember when you had to draw a map of Britain. Which side of Britain was Wales on?*

Finn closed his eyes, pictured the map, saw Wales bulging like a pregnant belly on the west side of Britain. 'West. So that means I have to go west. But which way's west?'

Which way does your bedroom window face?

'West. Towards where the sun goes down. So...' Finn paused, his forehead wrinkling in thought. Then he blurted out excitedly, 'Oh I get it. All I have to do is go towards the sun.'

That's right. Well done, said Zack. *And I'm sorry for calling you stupid. You're not stupid at all.*

Feeling pleased with himself, Finn squinted at the sun. It hung low above a cluster of glass and steel towers, the tallest of which narrowed at its peak to a needle point, upon which it seemed the sun would soon be impaled. He set off walking against the general flow of pedestrians. The towers loomed over him like glittering pillars of ice, blocking out the sun. Here and there, slender beams of sunlight found their way to the street. He followed them.

Beyond the towers, the round, red glare of the evening sun was revealed. Rush hour was over and there was an expectant lull in the streets as the city prepared itself for the night. Finn hurried onwards. His rucksack's straps seemed to be getting thinner and sharper with every step. He emptied it of all his school books and dumped them in a bin. That made him feel better all round. Half an hour later, the sun set behind the chimneys of the city, bathing everything in a cindery orange glow. He was in a residential area of big, posh-looking houses. Their neatly tended gardens made him think of Wales.

'I must be getting near the end of the city now,' he said. Zack made an unconvinced sound.

Then Finn came to the park. An expanse of grass crisscrossed by paths stretched away to a low, sparsely wooded hill that caught the last of the sun. He couldn't see beyond the hill. 'This is it, Zack,' Finn exclaimed. 'This is where the city stops and the countryside starts.'

He ran towards the hill. A fresh, clean smell replaced the city smell of exhaust fumes and clustered bodies. The noise of traffic faded to a murmur. Breathing hard, he climbed the hill. At its summit he came to a stop and let out a groan. On the far side of the hill there was more grass, but after a short distance it came to an end at a redbrick Victorian terrace. And beyond the terrace was rank after rank of houses, roads, apartment blocks, churches, offices, shops, car parks and all the rest of it. He whirled in a full circle. The city, the city, the city. It was the same wherever he looked. The sight sapped his strength, his will to go on. 'I'll never find my way out of this city,' he sighed.

Yes you will, said Zack. *You just think you won't because you need a rest and something to eat.*

Finn sat down against a tree. As the afterglow of the sun faded, he buttered some bread with his thumb and swallowed it with a few gulps of milk. A rustling sound from a nearby bush caught his attention. He suddenly became aware of the fast gathering shadows and the emptiness of the park. *It's just a bird or something,* Zack assured him.

'It doesn't sound like a bird,' said Finn, shoving the bread and milk back into his rucksack.

As Finn rose to leave, a figure emerged from behind the bush. It was a man—or at least, had the shape of one. He was wearing a filthy hooded sweatshirt with the hood up. Bloodshot eyes peered out over a foxy mass of whiskers that covered almost his entire face. He staggered towards Finn, who turned with a cry and sprinted away. Somewhere near the bottom of the hill, a dark shape buffeted into his thigh, twisting him sideways. He hit the ground hard and lay winded, unable to move. Something cold and damp touched his cheek.

'Douglas, no,' yelled a voice. 'Come away from him. Bad boy, naughty boy!'

A man came into view, holding a black Labrador by its collar. He was older than Finn's father, with grey hair, thick glasses and a thin, cleanly shaven face. He looked at Finn with concern. 'Are you okay? God, you're not okay, are you? Look at your knee.'

When the man said that, Finn noticed his knee hurt. 'Sit, Douglas,' the man commanded, and as the dog obeyed, he stooped to help Finn to his feet. Finn looked at his knee. His left trouser leg was torn and there was blood on his skin. He could feel more blood running warmly down the inside of his trousers. 'Can you walk?' the man asked.

Finn limped a few steps and nodded.

'Good. At least there's nothing broken,' said the man. 'Still, you should get that cut seen to. Do you live nearby?'

'No.'

'Are you here on your own?'

Finn was about to nod, but it occurred to him that maybe it would be best if the man didn't know he was alone. 'I was with some mates, but we got split up.'

The man glanced around, then his gaze returned to Finn. 'I tell you what. I live just over there.' He pointed to the terraced houses. 'I've got plasters and antiseptic cream and all that kind of thing at my place. I can fix up your knee for you there no problem.'

Finn looked at the man uncertainly. 'Mum said I should never go anywhere with strangers.'

'And Mum's absolutely right. But that cut needs looking after straight away. I bet it's hurting like mad, isn't it?'

Finn nodded. The cut hurt so bad it made him want to cry, and it was getting worse by the second. Douglas stood up suddenly, whining to continue his walk. Finn flinched backwards. He liked dogs, but big ones made him nervous. 'There's nothing to be scared of,' said the man. 'Douglas is as soft as a brush. You can stroke him, if you like. He won't bite.'

Gingerly, Finn reached out to stroke Douglas's head. His fur was soft and warm. 'See, he's very friendly,' said the man as Douglas's tail began to wag. 'That's why he jumped up at you. He just wanted to play.'

His confidence growing, Finn stroked down under Douglas's neck. The fur was even softer there, like velvet. Douglas's gums peeled back as though he was smiling, his rough tongue darted out to lick Finn's hands. The sensation was pleasurable in a cringe-making way. Finn almost smiled.

'My name's Stan,' said the man. 'What's yours?'

'Finn.'

'Well, Finn, now that we know each other's names, we're not strangers anymore, are we?'

'Suppose not.'

'So then, let's go and get that knee of yours patched up.'

Still hesitating, Finn glanced from Douglas to Stan and back. Stan put Douglas on his lead and held it out to Finn. 'Here, Finn, you walk him. It'll take you mind off your knee.'

Finn took the lead. At a command from Stan, Douglas started pulling strongly in the direction of the terrace. 'Keep him on a short lead, and he won't pull so much,' said Stan. 'Have you got a dog of your own?'

'No. Mum says there's not enough room in our flat for one.'

'That's a shame. Every little boy should have a dog.'

They walked on for a bit in silence, Finn concentrating on keeping Douglas under control. Then Stan said, 'Does your mum know where you are?'

'No.'

'Won't she be worried about you?'

Finn thought about his mum lying in bed, looking more like a dead person than a live one. He shrugged. 'I'm sure she would be if she knew you were here,' said Stan. 'I know it looks nice, but drunks, druggies, homeless people and...and other worse types frequent this park after dark. I wouldn't dare come in here without Douglas.'

They left the park, crossed a road and descended some steps to a basement-level door with 'Flat 1b' on it. Stan opened the door and stepped inside. Finn hesitated to follow, but Douglas jerked forward, dragging him into the hallway. 'You can let him off his lead,' said Stan.

Finn unclipped the lead and Douglas bounded off to lap thirstily at a bowl of water. Finn followed Stan into a living-room furnished with a battered old leather sofa and armchairs that spilled their stuffing. A small foldaway table was in front of the sofa; on top of it, a plate smeared with the remnants of some sauce. Numerous well-chewed bones and dog toys were scattered over the carpet, which was thickly covered with dog hair. The room's only window looked out onto a brick wall. 'Do you live here by yourself?' asked Finn.

'Yes, just me and Douglas. Sit yourself down.'

As Finn lowered himself onto the sofa, Stan moved to close the curtains. 'I'll just get the plasters and things,' he said, heading out of the room.

You shouldn't have come here, Zack hissed as soon as they were alone.

'Why not? Stan's nice.'

He might be pretending.

'No he isn't. Why would he be?'

Before Zack could say anything else, Stan returned with Douglas trotting along beside him. He set down a bowl of water, some cotton-wool, a box of plasters and a tube of Savlon. 'Roll you trouser leg up,' he said. Finn did so, wincing as the material rubbed against his wound. Stan dipped cotton-wool into the water and dabbed at Finn's knee. Finn sucked on his lip, not wanting to cry in front of Stan. To his relief, the cut didn't look half as bad once all the blood had been cleaned off. Stan slathered it with Savlon and stuck a plaster over it. 'There, that should do it,' he said. 'How does it feel?'

'Much better, thanks.'

'Good.' Stan retreated to an armchair, Douglas settled down at his feet. They both looked at Finn intently. 'So, Finn, are you going to tell me what you were doing in the park so late?'

'I was just messing about with my friends.'

Stan lifted a knowing eyebrow. 'Come on now, Finn, you can tell me and Douglas the truth. We won't tell anyone, I promise.'

Finn sat silent a long moment, chewing his lip, then he said, 'I'm going to Wales.'

'Wales! Where in Wales?'

Finn took the photo out of his rucksack and showed it to Stan. 'There.'

'Is that your dad?'

'Yes. He lives there. I'm going to live with him.'

'So let me get this straight, Finn. Your parents aren't together anymore, and you're running away to live with your dad.'

Finn's eyes grew round with surprise. 'How did you know that? I never said it to you.'

'You didn't have to. I was a little boy once, too, you know.' Stan pointed at the photo. 'How are you going to get there?'

'I'm walking.'

Stan guffawed. 'You can't walk to Wales.'

'Why can't I?' Finn asked a touch sullenly, needled by Stan's laughter.

'It's too far. You wouldn't even make it out of the city, never mind all the way to Wales.'

'Yes I would,' insisted Finn. 'The city doesn't go on forever.'

'It might as well do, as far as you're concerned.' Stan's eyes wandered away to take in the room—the grey tinged woodchip wallpaper, the tired-looking curtains. He sighed. 'Sometimes I think there's no way out of this city for any of us, except by a miracle.'

'It doesn't matter what you say, I've got to try anyway.'

'Things really that bad at home, huh?'

Finn made no reply, but the pain that pinched his forehead was answer enough.

'You know, Finn, if there's one thing I've learnt it's that sometimes there isn't any way out,' Stan motioned to the window, 'out there. Sometimes the only real way out is in. Do you understand what I'm talking about?'

'I think so,' Finn answered hesitantly. 'You mean in my head?'

'Kind of.' Stan looked at Finn as if trying to make his mind up about something. He rose suddenly and gathered up the bowl, cotton wool, plasters and Savlon. 'I'll explain some more when I've tidied these things away.'

The instant Stan—again followed by Douglas—was out of the room, Zack piped up, *You've got to run away from here right now.*

'Why?'

I don't like that man. He's too nice.

'How can someone be too nice?'

I don't know, but he is.

'Now you're the one being stup—'

Shh, Zack interrupted. *I hear a voice. Listen.*

They sat in silence, straining to hear. After a few seconds, they caught the sound of Stan's voice, too low to be clearly audible.

'He's probably just talking to Douglas,' Finn said, but he got up and padded into the hallway. Stan's voice came from behind a door at the far end of the hallway. Finn pressed his ear to it.

'Yes, that's right,' Stan was saying, almost in a whisper. 'Finn...I don't know...I'd say about ten, maybe younger.'

Finn's heart pushed up his throat, lodging there like a fist. *See*, said Zack. *I told you.*

Finn heard a low whine and a scratching sound on the door. 'Excuse me a moment,' said Stan. 'What is it, Douglas?'

Run, yelled Zack.

Finn ran for the front door, oblivious to the pain in his knee. Yanking it open, he scrambled up the steps. He dodged around a street corner, blinking as the cold night air licked his face, sprinting on and on past houses illuminated from without by the apricot glow of street lamps and from within by the steely flicker of televisions. Finally, gasping for breath, he came to a stop. He leant against a wall, feeling light headed and a little sick.

Keep going, keep going, urged Zack.

'But which way do I go?' Finn spread his hands to indicate that he no longer knew north from south, west from east.

I dunno, but you need to keep going.

Finn continued onwards, walking, running, then walking again. He hadn't gone much further when he spotted a figure up ahead. Instinctively, he jumped over a garden wall. He huddled down against it, trying to keep his breathing from sounding so loud. Minutes seemed to pass. There was no sound. 'Do you think it's okay to carry on?' he whispered.

Before Zack could reply, a familiar, heavily bearded face loomed over the wall. Eyes peered beadily down at Finn from inside a hood. The beard split open in a grin of crooked yellow teeth. 'Well, well, what 'ave we got 'ere, eh?' The voice was slurry at the edges. Finn recoiled from its sour alcohol stink. 'It's alright, young 'un, I ain't gonna hurt you.' The man grabbed Finn's arm and pulled him upright. 'I seen you in the park, didn't I?'

Finn nodded, too choked with fear to speak. Up close the man appeared even less manlike and more like some kind of animal.

'Who was that feller you went off with, your old man?'

Finn shook his head.

'So what is he then, some kind of perv? I'll bet he wanted you to toss him off or summat, didn't he? Yeah, course he did, the dirty old fucker.' The man chuckled. His tongue lolled out of his mouth, licking at the fringes of his beard as if seeking food. 'What've you got in your bag?'

'N-nothing,' Finn managed to stammer out.

'It don't look like nothing.' The man started to pull the rucksack straps off Finn's shoulders.

'Don't,' whimpered Finn, trying to get his arm free.

The man's grip tightened to the point of pain. 'Keep that up, little man, and you'll piss me off.'

Finn stopped struggling. The man released his arm to open the rucksack and root through it. 'What the fuck do you want with all this chicken soup?' he snorted. 'You got a cold or summat?'

'They're for my mum.'

'Well she's welcome to 'em. I fuckin' hate chicken soup.'

The man found the photograph. As he pawed it with his black-nailed fingers, a shudder of anger ran through Finn. He snatched for the photo, but the man lifted it out of his reach. 'Do that again and you'll get a slap,' he warned. He tapped the photo. 'That your dad, is it?'

Finn nodded.

'I fuckin' hate campin', me. Where was this taken?'

'Wales.'

'Wales!' The man spat a ball of phlegm onto the pavement. 'Sheep-shaggers' paradise. My old man used to make us suffer a couple of weeks there every summer when I were a kid.'

A spark of hope came into Finn's eyes. 'Please, mister, do you know where in Wales that is?'

The man eyed Finn curiously. 'Don't you remember?'

'No.'

'And what you so keen to know for?'

Reluctantly, Finn told the man about how he was trying to get to Wales to live with his dad. The man burst into laughter. 'A runaway, are you? Just like me. I ran away from home when I were fifteen. Best fuckin' thing I ever did.' The man squinted at the photo again and seemed to be studying it intently. 'Y'know what,' he said, 'I reckon I do know where this is.'

Finn's hope flared into excitement. 'Really? Where?' he asked in a quick, eager voice.

'Tell you what, I'll do you a deal,' the man said with a sly smile. 'You help me, and I'll help you find your old man.'

A warning sounded in Finn's brain, but his desire to find his dad overrode it. 'Okay.'

'Nice one.' The man gave Finn back his rucksack. To Finn's dismay, he put the photo in his pocket. 'I'll hold onto this until our deal is through. Right then, young 'un, follow me.'

The man led Finn through the streets, eyes flickering from side to side, never still for a second. 'What's your name, young 'un?' he asked.

'Finn.'

'Mine's Mister Fox.' With a chuckle, he added, 'At least, that's what me mates call me.'

Mister Fox stopped outside a semi-detached house, set well back from the street behind a tall yew-hedge. There were no lights on. Raising a finger to his lips, he approached a gate at the side of the house. He tried the latch and made a small satisfied sound when it opened, as if he'd expected it to be unlocked. At the rear of the house, he pointed to a tiny open window, some seven feet from the ground. 'I'll give you a boost and you climb inside and open the back door,' he whispered. 'The back door has a Yale lock. Do you know what that is?'

Finn nodded; the front door of their flat had a Yale lock, which made it easy to lock yourself out. His heart was beating faster than it ever had before. He knew he should turn and run, but he couldn't bring himself to abandon the photo, and with it, any hope of finding his dad. Mister Fox made a cradle with his hands. Finn put his foot in it and Mister Fox boosted him up to the window. He grabbed the frame, wriggled through the open window, and dropped to the floor. It was pitch dark inside the house. He could smell air freshener and, underneath it, a faint tang of fried onions. He felt his way forwards, fumbled at a door handle. Beyond the door was a hallway, dimly illuminated by the ambient glow of the city. He stood listening a second. There was no sound except his own rapid breathing. He crept to the back door. As he reached for the lock, Zack hissed, *Don't open it, he's a liar, he doesn't know where your dad is.*

'Be quiet, Zack,' Finn snapped.

But Zack wouldn't be quiet. He went on, anxious, pleading, *If you let him in, something really bad will happen. I know it. You have to get away from him. Please, Finn. Please, please listen.*

'I don't want to listen to you.' Finn's voice rose dangerously. 'I can't listen to you.' He opened the back door.

Mister Fox broke into a grin at the sight of him. 'Good lad.' He drew Finn by the arm to the front door, which had a window in it. 'Now you keep look out and give me a shout if any other fucker turns up.'

Finn peered through the glass, tensing at every passing car, while from upstairs came the sound of drawers being rifled through, mattresses being overturned, sheets being ripped and stuff being thrown around. After several minutes, Mister Fox reappeared, a bulging duvet cover slung over his shoulder. 'Come on, let's get the fuck out of here,' he said.

They slunk out of the house and through the streets, keeping to the shadows where possible. They ducked through a hole in a wire fence at the side of a railway bridge and scuttled across a yard of derelict train carriages. Mister Fox clambered into a carriage and hoisted Finn up after him. The interior of the carriage was wallpapered with graffiti and reeked of booze and vomit. Its seats were slashed and broken up. Mister Fox began taking things— jewellery, a laptop, a couple of iPods—out of the duvet cover. 'This is fuckin' classy stuff,' he said, more to himself than Finn.

He produced a bottle. 'Eighteen-year-old malt, finished in bourbon, sherry, and port wood for unparalleled taste quality,' he said, reading from the label. He unscrewed the top and took a long gulp. 'Oh-hh fuck, man that's good.' He took another swig. 'Fuck yes.' He held the bottle out to Finn. 'Here, little man, get some of this down your neck.'

'No thanks.'

Mister Fox's face twisted into a scowl. 'Don't you fuckin' "no thanks" me. No kid says "no thanks" to me.' He shoved the bottle into Finn's hands. 'When I say drink, you drink. Got it? Now drink!'

Finn put the bottle to his lips. He choked as the burning liquid hit his throat and tried to lower the bottle, but Mister Fox held it in place. 'Drink, you little prick, drink, drink, drink,' he chanted.

Finn felt the whiskey burn right through him, brand itself upon his stomach his brain. He jerked away from Mister Fox, retching. And Mister Fox fell back against a seat, laughing. Finn's head was buzzy. 'I...have...can...photo...' His words didn't seem to want to come out in the right order.

'What do you want? Is this what you want? Is this what you want?' taunted Mister Fox, waving the photo in front of Finn, who grabbed at it, missed and almost toppled over. Mister Fox laughed even louder. 'These kids today, eh? Can't take their fuckin' drink.'

'Please,' pleaded Finn. 'Please, please.'

'Alright. Here, have it and shut your fuckin' whining.'

Mister Fox tore the photo in two and chucked both halves on the floor. Letting out an anguished wail, Finn snatched them up. The photo was torn down the middle, him in one half, his dad in the other. His voice trembling with tears, Finn yelled at Mister Fox, 'You fuck...fuck you fucker!'

'What's your problem? It's only a photo.'

'You bastard,' Finn shrieked at the top of his voice. More words burst out of him like a long pent up torrent, 'You bastards. Fucker bastards. I hate you. I hate you both.' He was no longer talking to Mister Fox, his eyes were squeezed shut and in front of him he saw his parents. He flung himself at them, falling over, kicking and punching about on the floor in an out of control fit of rage. Gradually his wild flailing slowed and his voice dropped to a gasping, almost inaudible whisper. 'Hate...I hate...bastards...'

Mister Fox stood over him, bottle in hand. There was no pity in his eyes, but he shook his head. 'They really did a job on you, mate, didn't they?' He reached down to haul Finn to his feet. 'C'mon.'

'Where are we going?'

'You want out of this city, don't you? Well I'm gonna show you the way.'

Finn followed Mister Fox from the carriage, swaying from side to side, reeling and almost falling every few paces. They approached a fence, beyond which a steep gravel embankment descended to a railway track. Mister Fox pointed to the dark opening of a tunnel, into which the track disappeared. 'That goes straight as a shot under the city, all the way to the countryside. There's a walkway beside the tracks. You'll be alright as long as you stay on it.'

The tunnel yawned like a giant's mouth, with the train tracks its tongue. Even through the fug of alcohol, Finn felt fear swell up inside. 'I don't think I can go in there.'

'Course you can.' Mister Fox pressed a torch into Finn's hands. 'Believe me, little man, this is the only way out for you. Stay up here and you'll just get lost and end up walking in circles until the coppers or some dick eater or other scumbag picks you up.'

Mister Fox lifted the bottom of the fence. Finn squirmed under and, clutching the wire, pulled himself upright. 'You never told me where in Wales the photo was taken, Mister Fox.'

Mister Fox shrugged. 'Fucked if I know. But if you make it to there, don't ever, ever come back here. Do you hear?'

Finn nodded. He slid on his bum down the embankment. At the mouth of the tunnel, he glanced back. Mister Fox was gone. The tunnel exhaled a cool, dank breath in his face. He switched on the torch, aiming the thin beam of light into the darkness. There was a narrow walkway to the left of the track. 'Zack,' he whispered, as if afraid of waking some monster asleep in the tunnel. No reply. 'Please, Zack, I'm sorry for not listening.' Again, no reply. Heaving a sigh and swallowing a choking breath, Finn edged into the tunnel.

His legs still weren't working properly, so he groped a hand along the dirty, cobwebby walls for support. Within a few paces, the sounds of the city were deadened. In the silence he heard a dripping sound, although it was muffled and far away. And he thought he heard a scuttling and scuffling as of rats. He stood stiffly in the darkness, fighting an urge to flee the tunnel. For some reason, he recalled what Stan had said about how sometimes the only real way out was in. He found himself repeating that thought over and over again as he made his way deeper into the tunnel. The walls were slimy now and the walkway was slippery underfoot. Moss hung in ragged strands from the arched roof.

Onwards he went, walking as fast as he dared, on and on, deeper and deeper in, drawn forwards by the thought, *the only way out is in, the only way out is in, the only...*

A new sound silenced his thoughts. It started as a low rushing of air, away in the distance behind him, but quickly swelled to a deep, vibrating growl. He plugged his ears, but nothing could block it out. It got inside him, resonating along his bones, reverberating in his temples, like the roar of the wind outside his bedroom window. 'Go away and leave me alone,' he yelled. But the sound didn't go away, it grew and grew, until it seemed to come from every direction at once, so that he was stunned, bewildered, close to hysteria. He started running. Running, slipping, falling, scrambling to his feet, stumbling onwards, falling again, banging his head. Lights were blaring all around now, as well as the noise, the thunderous noise. There was an instant, like a sharp intake of breath, then he felt himself being lifted up high in the air and carried away in the arms of the noise. Everything was rushing by, colours blurring, mixing. He wasn't in the tunnel anymore. Behind him was the dim outline of a sprawl of buildings. In front, as far as he could see, nothing but fields. Ten, twenty, fifty miles passed with the speed of a thought. And then finally, suddenly, he was there. In Wales. Sat next to his dad in that nameless place between the hill and the sea. The two of them smiling. His mum smiling back as she raised the camera to take their photo.

The anxiety of impending fatherhood is a common subject for short stories, but it's one of those personal events that can be difficult to translate well into fiction. Fortunately, Adrian Stumpp has provided us with an example of how it can be done.

Nativity

Adrian Stumpp

Ever since we bought a house in the suburbs, I haven't been able to sleep. I have nightmares I can't remember. I wake in dread and a sweated fever with my heart knocking like a sick engine, and drink several glasses of water straight from the tap before my hands stop shaking. I feel like nothing belongs to me and all the time I catch myself wondering how the hell I got here, who is this woman in bed next to me, and I know the house is part of it.

The house makes no sense to me. It is too big and I don't know how to use it. The house is a decade-old rambler with a dishwasher and a stainless steel refrigerator with dispensers in the door for filtered water and ice, crushed or cubed, whichever your pleasure. I'm thirty-five years old and never until now has my life required a preference for crushed or cubed ice. Not that it matters, because I still drink water from the faucet, the harder the better. Soft water gives me a skin rash, I've discovered. Something else I never worried about before living in this house.

My wife is having a baby. She gets mad when I tell people this. She thinks I should say 'we' are having a baby, but in truth, she will do it from here out. My only essential responsibility has already been performed, with much gusto, and after browsing the important baby books she's given me, I can tell you with extreme confidence my job was the best part of the process.

For a long time I told her we couldn't have a baby. They're too expensive. I was going to school and only kept a part-time job, and then I was unemployed and uninsured throughout my post-graduate studies. There were obscene student loans and it took a while to find a teaching job and a while longer to find a position as permanent faculty. Our apartment had lead paint on the walls and asbestos in the ceiling and it was too small and located in a bad neighbourhood.

After all these excuses were gone I couldn't think of any more, and like the street-barker of a Las Vegas massage parlour, Amy tempted me with endings happier than those found in a latex reservoir, and now she's nine months pregnant. The baby could come any day, Amy threatens me; it will in fact be here no later than Friday, December twenty-seventh, when her doctor will induce labour if the baby hasn't already.

The doctor seems convinced the baby will be born on Christmas, just to spite him. He is a portly man in his early fifties who rides a Harley-Davidson. The baby is his arch nemesis. It took three separate ultrasound appointments before the baby would cooperate enough for the doctor to discern a gender. The baby has rendered all of the doctor's sage predictions inept. It has changed genders once and shuffled its conception date by one and then two weeks, before dropping into Amy's pelvis a week early. The doctor grits his teeth and laughs and pretends not to harbour any irrational animosity towards our baby, but I know he is the only person whose ambivalence exceeds my own. Now he is determined to keep the baby in there until after Christmas. He has modified Amy's diet, her exercise habits, and even our sexual practices. He says these measures ought to do the trick but so far every confrontation with the baby has ended in failure for the doctor.

Pregnancy has been generous to Amy. Her stretch marks are not deep and she protects them from scarring with expensive lotions. Her ankles swelled but not so much that she can't wear shoes, and the hair on her legs has virtually stopped growing now that she can't reach to shave them, which I've been told is the opposite of what usually happens. She glows, a habit of the knocked up. She didn't suffer morning sickness, not even in the beginning. The only adverse reaction she has had to pregnancy is sleep-punching. I have started lying to my colleagues and students in order to protect her. I don't want them to know my wife beats me in her sleep.

I didn't always fear the house. When we bought it, I was excited to finally have my own room. I had never had my own room before. I went from sharing with my half-brother to foster-brothers to dorm-mates to Amy. I filled my room with a couple bookcases and a centrefold pin-up and a desk under the window where I would correct student papers in the evenings. Then Amy got pregnant and evicted me. Now my room has clouds and birds and frogs painted on the walls, and a matching crib and dresser, and a plastic table set with chairs shaped like toadstools. Amy said she needed my room for the baby because it was close, right across the hall from the master bedroom. She said I should be hanging out in the garage anyway, since that's what men do. The garage is paved in a slick black shell, made of what I don't know, though I understand it's to keep oil from staining the underlying concrete.

For a while I spent my evenings in the garage comfortable enough—it's heated—polishing my tools and staring at my Honda and Amy's Nissan and longing for one of them to need fixing. But the garage is not for me. It reminds me more of an airplane hangar than a garage. It is too empty and the ceilings are too high. It echoes, and spending too much time out there makes me feel lonely. Sometimes I would wander the neighbourhood, politely knocking on garage doors, to see what the other men did in their garages. Looking for ideas. Some of them have pinball machines or mini-bars or putting greens or televisions mounted to the wall so they can watch NASCAR on Sunday afternoons. One guy suggested I buy a speed boat, but I don't know anything about boats. I've never been in one before, I wouldn't even know how to get it in the water, and I suspect you need a special license to drive a boat.

My new room is on the opposite side of the house and the window above my desk looks onto the street. After calming myself from a nightmare, I put a few ice cubes in a tumbler with some whiskey. For a while I experimented with crushed ice, but found the rye snow-cone didn't agree with me. Amy used to buy bottles of red wine from a California vineyard because she said a glass of wine at the dinner table was less alarming to company than straight shots of cheap hooch. But the wine was terrible stuff; I could barely choke it down. I don't care how much it costs or what flavours it's supposed to accentuate, I like my bottom-shelf rot-gut just fine.

I sit at my desk sipping whiskey, smoking a joint, and looking out the window until eight in the morning. It's light enough outside to see, just a little before sunrise, and the snow is tinted the pink of steamed skin. The lamppost on the corner still hasn't turned off, but already the first Sunday morning joggers cruise the sidewalk beneath my window, bundled in running suits and ear warmers and streaming rime from their nostrils. It hasn't snowed for a few days, but the temperature won't raise enough to melt what is already there, it just hardens and cracks like slurry on the lawn. Downstairs I hear cupboards banging in the kitchen and I open the window to pitch the roach into a snow bank and wave the smoke and stink out with a sweater I flap like a flag in two hands.

Yesterday Amy told me she wanted a dog. I said she was already getting a baby to play with, she didn't need a dog. A baby and a dog would be two more mouths to feed and I'm a nervous wreck as it is. She said the dog wasn't for her, it was for the baby. I said we didn't even know if the baby likes dogs, maybe the baby is a cat person. But Amy is convinced there's something wrong with you if you don't like dogs, it's a sure sign of a bad person, and maybe she's right. Maybe I am a bad person, that's something I hadn't worried about yet. I said no to the dog but I know we'll end up getting one, and so does Amy. Already she and the baby conspire against me. Amy spends a lot more time with the baby than I do and can apparently divine its opinion of any number of things. The baby always votes with Amy. The marijuana is a good example. Amy never minded my smoking until she was having a baby. Now suddenly it's a bad thing. The baby doesn't like it. Amy doesn't want it in the house. Child Protective Services will steal our baby if they find out.

Officially, I don't know if the baby is a boy or girl. I'm just supposed to think it's a baby. I didn't want to know before the birth, I wanted it to be a surprise, but every time Amy returns from the store she shows me the overalls and dump trucks and blue onesies and baseball-printed bibs she's bought. Amy is lousy at keeping secrets, but she thinks she's keeping this one and I don't want to spoil it for her.

I worry the baby will stick a butter knife in a light socket and fry himself. I have already put plastic stoppers in all the outlets, but I know sometimes babies figure out how to take them out. I worry he will fall down the stairs or drown in the toilet. I worry he will suffocate in his sleep or have an allergic reaction to his vaccination shots or develop autism or acute dyslexia. I worry he will be born with four toes or six fingers or his heart on the outside of his lungs. I worry he will be gay, not that I would mind—I wouldn't—but I know the world can be very cruel to homosexuals and I would just as soon see him avoid that, if at all possible. I worry he will get addicted to methamphetamine or disco music or Jesus. I worry he might vote Republican. Most of all, though, I worry he will someday hate me with the same passion with which I hated my own dad.

My dad ruined my mother's marriage to her previous husband, and when I was four he ran out on us. I never saw or heard from him again. Mom didn't leave her bed for weeks. She cut her wrists. She tried to go back to her first husband, but my conception had sufficiently mutilated any chance of that happening.

She tried to hold it together and for a while did a pretty good job. She was on welfare a few years, and then she worked three jobs and continued sharing custody of my half-brother and two half-sisters. I didn't know anything about my dad because every time I would ask about him, Mom would cry and lock herself in her room, so I stopped asking. I learned to hate him slowly, not from Mom, but from seeing other kids who had dads and how having dads made them different than me, like they were learning things from their dads I had no access to. They didn't have to know me too well to tell I had something important missing. I hated those kids and I hated their dads and I hated my dad, too.

Mom never recovered from it. Her depression worsened over the next four years. At times I could feel her struggling against it, clawing to somehow right her scuttled life—other times she dove to it and hell sounded to her bottom fathom. I used to think she couldn't get over my dad, but now I think what she couldn't get over was her own poor taste. At some point in her life she'd had to choose between the father of her children and the man who would become my father. She made the wrong choice and the knowledge of it tortured her, and of course, all the time there I was, the constant reminder of her great regret, smiling and smiling and unbeknownst to me, damning her all the time.

But it was only that I loved you. You were a good mom sometimes, and you never left me. You whipped me with a water-hose so hard the brass nozzle left scars on my back Amy can sink her whole thumb into. You locked me in a closet for sixteen hours and then hit me in the head for shitting myself. You didn't feed me for days because you spent our grocery money on heroin and you fucked drug dealers while I watched cartoons on the front-room floor, but you never left me. They had to send cops to the apartment to throw you cuffed and face-down on the landing in front of the housing project, wailing profanities at me. They hauled me off to foster care in a police cruiser, and I want you to know I wouldn't have gone except they had corndogs and I was starving. You said you should've taken a coat-hanger to me when you had the chance, you called me a mistake, but you were my mother, and I loved you.

The next night Amy hits me again, and this is the worst yet, because I hurt her. She hits me in the cheek with her fist so hard she wakes up sobbing.

I say sorry and ask if she's okay. It takes a minute for the strobe light to get out of my skull before I can figure out what happened. She sprained her wrist, or I guess I sprained her wrist, and we wrap it in an Ace bandage. My cheekbone bruises the purple of a gin blossom. Monday I confide to the chair of my department. I want her to understand the situation so she doesn't think my lying is symptomatic of battered-husband syndrome or something.

A couple weeks before we found out about the pregnancy, Amy started grinding her teeth nights. Hard. I have been known to sleep through a carjacking outside my window or a drug sting down the hall, but a sound like the obliteration of tectonic plates in bed next to me is something else. There's nothing like it. Listening to it makes your jaw hurt. I woke her, but it did no good. As soon as she was asleep it would start again, like she was chewing gravel. Around the second trimester she stopped grinding her teeth and started decking me. At first, it was no big deal. She'd turn over in bed and wop me in the ear with a loose fist. 'Ouch, you hit me,' I'd say. 'Sorry,' she'd slur with no great sincerity, and be out again. She split my chin open six weeks later. I told people I cut myself shaving. A month after, she blackened my right eye—I fell down the stairs.

I asked Amy's doctor if he'd ever heard of pregnant women punching their husbands for no apparent reason, a hormone imbalance causing aggressive chemicals to be released in the brain, something like that. He said it happens all the time. I asked if it ever happens while the wife is in deep sleep, stage four let's say. Curiosity. Never mind the ripe olive where my right eye used to be. I might have a friend who would like to know. The doctor referred me to his sister-in-law, a marriage counsellor. But Amy refuses to see a marriage counsellor because she's afraid the therapist would decide our problems, such as they might be, are entirely my fault, and that's something Amy doesn't think I need to hear right now. She knows I've been having a difficult time with the move and the new job and now a baby on the way.

Amy says I'm going through poverty withdrawals. She thinks the nightmares are symptomatic of detox.

Now my left cheek swells so bad my eye has no peripheral vision. There's a black spot in my line of sight—I can't see over my engorged zygoma. 'The damnedest thing,' I tell the department secretary, 'I slipped in the shower and did a face-plant on the wall tile. Just clumsy. Looks worse than it really is. Don't touch it, though.'

Later I sit at my desk, staring out the window, thinking about my son, and also my dad and my hatred of him. When Amy first got pregnant I worried I might someday leave her and the baby like my dad left me. I couldn't imagine ever doing such a thing, or even wanting to, but that didn't mean I never would. I feared it like Alzheimer's or prostate cancer, a dormant predisposition in my genes set to go off when I reached a certain age. Amy assured me that would never happen. I'm not the type. Abandonment is the last thing she fears. But you never know.

A dozen or so carollers in rubber galoshes and nylon snowsuits serenade the house across the street. Carollers are another thing I've never seen before; I didn't think they actually existed outside of movies. Some carry thermoses and some wear amazing Technicolor dream-scarves around their necks. Every house on our block is lit up like a whorehouse and a gentle snow falls straight down the windless night and through the snow the Christmas lights look acrylic and smoky. The snow plays tricks with the shadows of cars and buildings, as if the darkness itself were solid. The people who live in the house across the street are Jehovah's Witnesses but they don't seem to mind the carollers.

Several years ago I received a call from my oldest half-sister, Joanna, whom I hadn't talked to in ages. Mom had been arrested for cheque fraud and was being held in state custody as a flight risk until the trial. In Mom's things Joanna found an address for a Tom Devereaux of Plainview, Texas. She thought I probably wouldn't want it, but didn't think the decision hers to make. I took down the address and didn't think much of it other than to wonder how Mom had come into it, since when I was young she'd had no idea where he was.

Last December, shortly before we bought the house, I presented a paper at a conference at Texas Tech. Lubbock is not far from Plainview, and on a whim Amy suggested I might look up my dad.

The first thing he said was, 'Are you Ed or Eddy or Edward?' I told him I was Ed to pretty much everyone but my students, who called me Dr Devereaux, and my wife, who called me Edward. He wanted pictures and I showed him a dog-eared wedding photo I kept in my wallet and he seemed pleased with that. Tom had a long white scar across his upper lip, just beneath the septum, that ended at the corner of his mouth. Reconstructive surgery to repair a hair-lip he'd been born with, something I never knew about him.

Tom didn't try to hug me or even shake hands. He never touched me. He didn't apologize or offer excuses or grand speeches about making up for lost time. He just said it was damn good to finally see me, and I believed him—even more than the fear and shame, it seeped from every crease in his face.

He offered me macaroni and cheese with hotdogs, as well as the Dairy Queen up the road, both of which I declined. I accepted a Tecate and he brought me a whole case. I asked if he would join me and he said he'd been sober now nine years and still took meetings twice a month. He'd bought the beer special for me, which was fine—I had already decided to get drunk enough for both of us. I didn't think my mom was any of his business so when he asked how she was, I said she was doing great, and at some point I asked if he would mind telling me how he met my mother.

He'd been to a party earlier that midsummer night in 1973, and blitzed out of his mind on cocaine wandered into the Beck Street 7-11 in Salt Lake City, where my mom worked the graveyard shift.

It was a little after two a.m. on a weekday and the place had been empty since eleven o'clock and would stay that way at least another three hours. He thought her cute and flirted with her. She didn't say much, just grinned at his antics and played with a Coke straw between her teeth. He asked for her number. She said no, she didn't go on dates. He asked why not. She said she had three kids, her kids were her life, she didn't have time for stupid games. Tom bought a dime cigar, saved it for later, and asked her for a cigarette. She indicated the wax cup half full of water and stubs next to the cash register, but he preferred smoking outside.

The night was pleasant—very dry but not too hot—and he enjoyed the effect upon his blasted synapses. A dragonfly kept landing on Mom's hand and wouldn't leave her alone and she made him press his hand to hers and together they watched the dragonfly walk from one hand to the other.

Mom said, 'You're cute.'

Tom said, 'Back at ya.'

Inside, Tom said he would be in the bathroom if she cared to join her. She giggled and said that was probably the last thing she ought to do. He came back to say there was no soap. The soap was kept in a locked cabinet beneath the sink and he followed her into the bathroom where he kissed her from behind on the neck. In his memory the bathroom was barely big enough for two people and quite seedy with fingerprints on the mirror, stained porcelain, naked light bulb swinging on a cord overhead. They made out for a while and then he asked if she would suck him and she did. After, she had to check the store for customers and told him to wait. When she came back she peeled off her panties and hitched her mini-skirt over her hips and mounted him on the toilet bowl.

'Hi,' she said.

Every once in a while she had to pull her skirt back down and rearrange her bra to check the store for customers, and he waited in the bathroom for her to resume the ride. 'I have something I need to tell you,' she said, 'But first you have to promise you'll let me finish.'

He promised.

'I'm married,' she said.

Wobbling back into the front of the store, he felt embarrassed and a little guilty. The cocaine had gone to his stomach, and all things considered, he thought it about time to bail. He bought a pack of cigarettes and left without looking back.

Tom despaired recounting this tale. It embarrassed him and made me uncomfortable, but I needed to hear it. The story stirred something primal and familiar, and harangued something ancient in me toward self-awareness. It seemed to possess the bizarre logic of myth, my own personal creation myth, for it told me what I was and from whence I came. Several times Tom stopped, not wanting to continue, desperate to avoid my questions. I wanted the details, no matter how sordid, and several times interrupted the narrative to probe Tom for the weather, the bathroom scenery, the exact words exchanged.

After that night, Tom had a hard time putting Mom out of his thoughts. You can imagine the impression she must have made. Two months later he stumbled back into the 7-11, this time sober, on the off chance she might be working. Mom had held out a week before confessing to her husband, who'd filed for divorce a month before Tom came back. My parents married six weeks later before a justice of the peace. He was twenty-five and she two years older. That was November. I would be born in seven months, on June 24, 1974.

The carollers have moved to the next house on the street. Amy comes in to say she's just baked cookies if I want some, and to ask what I'm up to.

'Worrying.'

'What about?'

'If I'm going to leave you and the baby.'

'This again?' she asks and tries not to grin.

'What if I wake up one day and decide I can't do it anymore? What if I can't think about anything but getting out of here? What if I'm miserable and mediocre and domesticated and...basically middle class, and I hate my life, and I bolt?'

Amy giggles. 'I promise you won't do that. I know you.'

'But you can't know for sure,' I point out, 'It scares me.'

'I wish there was something I could do to ease your mind. I guess you'll just have to trust me.'

Amy runs her hand through my hair, the same way my mom did when I was little.

'What would happen if I left you and the baby?'

Amy shrugs. 'I'd be okay.'

'And the baby?'

'The baby would be okay too, I guess. Not great, but okay.'

She studies my face a few moments and knows something's still wrong. 'What is it?' she asks.

'And—would I be okay?'

I wake from a nightmare and Amy looms over me, sitting up in bed, still asleep. The shock snaps me upright. 'Christ, you scared me!' I say, 'Are you alright?' She cocks her right arm to her ear and I say, a little shriller than I care to admit, 'Amy. Hold—' and before I can finish she breaks my nose. I know it is broken before the blood even starts. We spend the first several hours of Christmas Eve in the emergency room. They give me a bandage and a prescription for painkillers and an opaque shield that straps around my face like a Halloween mask. I have to breathe through my mouth and my voice sounds thick and congested. Amy is beside herself with remorse and I don't discourage her. We had plans to brunch with my department chair and her husband, but I call to cancel and explain what happened. She calls back an hour later with the number and address of a nearby shelter for battered women. I feel drugged and humiliated and sore and am very much aware of how ridiculous I look. Walking out to the hospital parking lot, Amy asks for the fifth time this morning if there's anything she can do.

'I think you've done enough for one day,' I tell her, and tears brim her eyes. By the time we reach the car she can barely stand. She doubles over the baby, gasping; she appears to be embracing a beach ball under her dress. False contractions, she explains: I've upset her, and now the sight of me makes her dilate.

Amy slumps to the asphalt and cries. She can't move. I sprint back to the hospital to get an orderly with a wheelchair and Amy is admitted. The birthing room is not unlike our bedroom. The wallpaper looks like something Amy might pick out and the floorboards and shelves and furniture are made of an expensive looking pale wood.

Amy says not to worry, nothing's wrong with the baby, she could tell if it was time and it's not. She says it will stop if I just leave the room, take a walk or something, she can't stand the sight of me right now.

A Santa Claus in the maternity ward commons rings a silver bell and takes donations for the Salvation Army. I give a dollar, and another, and then a five-dollar bill. 'God bless,' Santa says, 'Merry Christmas.'

'Go to hell.'

Nearby I find a nativity scene. The plaster statues are three feet tall and hand painted. The parents kneel under a wooden awning and between them the miracle lies in a trough that's bursting straw from the seams. Kings and Magi stand by, their camels laden with chests of chocolate coins wrapped in gold foil and bushels of incense bound in twist ties with MADE IN CHINA printed on them. Fibreglass snow aglow with a string of white lights spills like foam over the adoring company.

When I visited Tom Devereaux last December I asked why he never came to see me, never called, never wanted anything to do with me as a child. He took me to his garage, where he pulled a staircase out of the ceiling by a cord and dug through some cardboard boxes in the loft above the garage until he found the one he wanted to show me.

'Open it,' he said.

The box was full of birthday cards and letters and unopened Christmas presents, all marked return to sender.

'All stuff I sent you,' he said. 'Your mom said you didn't need it. She said you didn't want anything of mine, said you hated me. I kept sending it, just in case you changed your mind. She kept returning it. Those were different times. Nowadays you hear about fathers demanding their rights. See their kids. Those were different times, is all. Your mom wanted me to give up my legal rights, so I did that. I could see why you must've hated me, is all. I thought it best to leave well enough alone.'

By the time I left I'd polished off three-quarters of a case of Tecate. Tom offered to put me up for the night but I didn't see any reason for that. There was no talk of future meetings, no promises to keep in touch, nothing like that. I gave him the wallet photo of me and Amy. He could've framed it on the wall or put it in his wallet or tucked it in the pages of an old book and forgotten about it. None of these would have surprised me. I drove the hour from

Plainview back to Lubbock on a lonely interstate between three and four in the morning. I was conscious of swerving a little but on the whole felt pretty fine. But when I arrived in the parking lot of my hotel I opened the rental car door and vomited on my shoes. How much of it the beer and how much subtler poisons, I was in no state to discern.

The hospital keeps Amy overnight as a precaution. A nurse found me looking at the nativity scene and told me Amy would be able to come home, but as soon as she sees me her uterus throws another tantrum until I leave the room.

The phone rings at 12:29. Amy has gone into labour and the doctor is on his way. Outside fat snowflakes drift like chick down. The night is clear and crisp and quiet and every house on the street glows the bright colours of television commercials. At the hospital Amy sits up in bed, naked but for a paper sheet, spitting air like a bellows. A boyish-looking nurse in pink scrubs tells me contractions are ninety seconds apart. Between bouts Amy says the IV makes her nauseous. It's supposed to induce labour, but Amy's cervix isn't thinning enough for her water to break and the nurse thinks they might have to break it for her. My job is to stay out of the way and speak to Amy in a soothing voice: 'Breathe,' I say, 'Choose a focal point. Squeeze my hand. Try to relax.'

An enormous man enters and shakes both our hands and introduces himself as Dr. Sreenivasan the anaesthesiologist. He makes me sign a form promising not to sue him if he kills my wife. He tells me to sit on a stool next to the bed and pull Amy's arms down while she braces her feet against my knees so he can stab her in the spine with a broadsword he calls a hypodermic needle. Amy stiffens and sighs and promises it wasn't that bad, but I know she's just saying that so I'll stop crying.

Thirty minutes later, the nurse checks Amy's dilations and tells us it looks like they'll have to manually break Amy's water. The nurse's bedside manner reminds me of a pancakes server at a late night diner. She explains the procedure to us. She tries to sound upbeat, as though it's routine, nothing to worry about, but to me she just seems excited to stab my wife in the vagina. She pages the obstetrician and exits and I toss a reassuring smile to Amy. 'Don't be scared,' Amy says, 'I'll be here with you.'

The nurse returns with a bus tub and a handful of napkins and an eighteen-inch medieval crochet hook. There is a muffled pop and the water spurts and sounds like a man urinating as it drains into the bus tub. Amy asks if I'm okay but I'm too woozy to answer. The doctor enters after all the hard work is done, introduces the intern who will observe, and parks himself on a stool between Amy's thighs. He buries his hands wrist deep and Amy's genitals stretch and split in a way I wouldn't have thought possible and two pushes later I have a son. The doctor fingers the baby's mouth and sticks a sucker in his nose and gives him a rough once-over with a towel to remove the cottage cheese. I cut the umbilical cord and they wrap him in a towel and I stand there dazed, pale, exhausted, and red eyed from weeping, and hold my son. Next, they give him to Amy and after her vital signs are checked we have our first family picture with the doctor. In the photograph the doctor looks bored and Amy looks beautiful. The face shield makes me look like the serial killer from a '70s B-movie. The doctor glares at the adversary who has ruined his Christmas morning, shakes my hand, tells Amy she did great, and rides his Harley back to his eggnog.

And then, Christmas afternoon, the three of us are alone—me, Amy, and our son, Thomas. He has a mouth like a cat's, split in the middle, where the two lobes of his face have partly fused—a hair-lip. He is very small and bright purple. His whole body quivers, expands, contracts, like a vital organ exposed to the open air, like a still-beating heart ripped from the body. He is my heart, drawn from Amy's body. He is the most fragile thing I have ever seen, but I know soon enough that will change. He will incubate and callus, until years from now his own heart will finally be hard enough to break.

'Are you still scared you might leave?' Amy teases me.

I thought it mattered where I came from. I thought the story of my origin could tell me something about who I am, and when I heard the story I thought it meant something. Thomas's eyelashes flutter and in his sleep his mouth sucks. He is teaching me a new story, one I have been preparing to learn. It is the myth of the orphan father. I am the man without parents who himself became a parent, the man with no beginning who is the beginning—and also the end. My mother was once as vulnerable and willing a newborn as my son, a long time ago, before whoever taught her to pour her pain into me had poured their pain into her. But Thomas will not know her pain because I will not teach it to him. I wish our roles had been reversed, that I had been the father and she my daughter, because I would have loved her better; I would have kept her safe.

'Promise me something,' I tell Amy, and the two of us make a promise. A covenant of semen and egg and DNA and cellular division, for nine months ossified and nourished with placenta and amniotic blood and water. We swear to each other, on our lives, on our immortal souls, on the stars and the moon and our mothers' names, we swear to be protectors.

For more information on the contributors
to this volume, please visit our website:

www.thefictiondesk.com/authors